SILVER FOX'S SECRET BABY

LYDIA HALL

ALSO BY LYDIA HALL

Series: Spicy Office Secrets

New Beginnings || Corporate Connection || Caught in the Middle || Faking It For The Boss || Baby Makes Three || The Boss's Secret || My Best Friend's Dad || Corporate Heat

Series: The Wounded Hearts

Ruthless Beast || Merciless Monster || Devilish Prince || Relentless Refuge || Vicious Vows || Lethal Lover || Sinister Savior || Wicked Union

Series: The SEAL's Protection

Guarded by the SEAL || Protected by the SEAL || Saved by the SEAL || Rescued by the SEAL

Series: The Big Bad Braddock Brothers

Burning Love || Tell Me You Love Me || Second Chance at Love ||
Pregnant: Who is the Father? || Pregnant with the Bad Boy

Series: The Forbidden Attraction

My Mommy's Boyfriend || Daddy's Best Friend || Daddy Undercover ||
The Doctor's Twins || She's Mine || Tangled Trust || Passion || Got to
be You

Series: Corrupt Bloodlines

Dangerous Games || Dangerous Refuge || Dangerous Obsession ||
Dangerous Vengeance || Dangerous Secrets

BLURB

Four years ago, he was my everything.
My mentor. My lover. My future.
Until scandal tore us apart.

Now, Dr. Ethan Mathews is back in my life.
Brilliant physician. **Silver fox**. *Forbidden temptation*.
And my new colleague at Mountain View Medical Center.

I thought I'd moved on, built a new life.
But one smoldering look, and I'm right back where I started.

There's just one thing he doesn't know:
The consequence of our past passion.
A secret with his eyes and my smile.

When old flames reignite and truths surface...
Will it mend our broken hearts or shatter us beyond repair?

★ *Lose your heart to this sizzling medical romance! A brilliant silver fox doctor, his determined protégée, and the secret baby that could change everything. Available now on Kindle Unlimited!* ★

1

LILY

Ethan's searing kiss before rolling off my sweat-soaked body was almost painful. The ache of knowing our short time tonight was over carved out a hollow spot inside me, and I whimpered when he pulled away.

"You don't really have to go back yet, do you?" I reached for him, letting my hand trail down his side and rest on his thigh as he sat on the edge of the narrow lower bunk in the doctors' on-call room. He glanced at me over his shoulder and smirked as he pulled off the full condom and tied it in a knot.

"Lily, I could stay here all night, but eventually, someone is going to walk in those doors, and you know what that would mean for us." I watched him stand and collect the empty foil wrapper from the condom. He walked to the trash can to discard them, and I rolled to my side to admire his toned curves. Twelve years older than me but with the body of a thirty-year-old... just looking at him made me want him again.

"Please, just a few minutes..." I patted the bed, and he turned. His eyes flicked to the door before returning to meet my gaze, and he sighed and picked up his boxers.

"A few..."

The tiny room was lit by a small lamp in the corner, not enough light to read by, but enough to enjoy the intimate moment. The glaring overhead fluorescent lighting was off for now, my choice. I preferred to make love in the dark when we rendezvoused here. Ethan preferred to not even think of our ethical indiscretions while on the hospital campus, but after the past nine months of frolicking and getting to know each other, I'd gotten him to loosen up.

"Mmm." I pulled him in as he lay back down beside me, this time with boxers on. His face still smelled like my sex, which wasn't at all a turn off to me. Though lately, smells had been making me a bit nauseous. "You are incredible, Dr. Matthews." Draping my arms around him, I brushed my lips across his and enjoyed the faint, salty flavor of my skin on him.

"We're taking risks, Lily." His voice was low and gravelly, a firm warning to me that he felt uneasy, but his hands groped my body, making sure there wasn't even enough space for air to slither between us.

When he deepened the kiss, I rolled to my back and the mattress groaned under our combined weight. His body crushed my breasts, which were very tender, and I felt love welling up in my chest, making me teary-eyed. I'd done a lot of that lately—get teary-eyed. At first, I chalked it up to work stress, but with the added breast tenderness and now the nausea, I knew it could only mean one thing. But I was waiting.

If a baby was on the horizon, I wanted to announce it in a special way. Besides, the residency hours hadn't been easy, and I barely had time to eat, let alone run to a pharmacy for a test.

"So, this weekend... You want to go to dinner somewhere?" I asked, lacing my hands through his short brown hair peppered with strands of silver. It was distinguished and attractive. Despite being older, Ethan still had the entire package—great looks, amazing personality, fantastic sexual drive, and everything about him made me want him more.

"I like that idea... Though we have to be careful—"

"I know," I said, interrupting. He didn't need to finish his sentence in order for me to get the point. He reminded me relentlessly that we were going against hospital policy. As a resident, I was prohibited from dating any doctor on staff, let alone my boss, but he and I hit it off so well. It was impossible to resist flirting with him, and one thing led to another, and now we were here, tangled in each other and sneaking around behind the administrations' backs.

"I just thought..." I let my voice trail off. Ethan and I agreed early on that we'd divulge our relationship once my first year was up and I was put on someone else's team. Sadly, HR didn't accept my transfer request, and short of going to a different hospital entirely, I was stuck reporting to him for another full year, which meant keeping what we had going a secret for even longer. I couldn't even articulate to him how much that depressed me.

"I'm sorry, baby. It's for the best." Ethan curled a strand of my curly hair around my ear and kissed my forehead. "I promise you, it will be worth it. We're doing so well right now. I'm not ashamed to make the world know you're mine, and I love you, but both of us rely on our jobs here..."

His logic was sound, but I still disliked it. And if I really was pregnant, it was going to change things in the near future, anyway. Ethan might think differently about the situation then. I just didn't want to get him all excited if a test showed I wasn't pregnant. So I'd wait a bit longer. Dinner this weekend would be a good time to talk to him.

I sucked in a breath and sighed. "Yes, it will be worth it. Eventually... someday." Having him in my arms right now, though, was my consolation. "And then we'll have forever." He hadn't proposed yet, but we had talked at length about a life together, having a child—at least one. He wanted to have a son to carry on his family name. I wanted a little girl. If I was pregnant, I didn't care what the sex was, as long as they were healthy.

"So, this weekend?" I prodded, again whining as he rolled off the bed.

"Yes. My place. You know the drill." He reached for his pants and shirt, then tossed mine at me. I'd only just clocked off. I hadn't even changed out of my scrubs yet, and we couldn't keep our hands off each other.

"Yes, love. I'll park in the back and come in through the kitchen." Sitting up, I took my scrubs from him and saw my bra and panties on the floor by the table across the room where this all started.

I slid off the bed and tiptoed toward my underwear, and the door burst open. I gasped, using my scrubs to cover myself as the light flicked on and Dr. Hayward gawked at me. His jaw dropped, then his forehead creased as he turned to look at Ethan.

"What the..." Hayward was only a few years older than me but a stickler for rules. And finding me completely naked, hiding behind my wadded-up scrubs, and Ethan with only his slacks on, was probably like striking gold for him. I saw the smirk before he spoke. "Naughty little doctors, aren't you?"

"Jack, please..." Ethan spoke first, reaching out toward his colleague, and all I could do was back toward the kitchenette area and whimper in shame. We weren't supposed to get caught.

"Looks like Dr. Matthews has some explaining to do..." Dr. Hayward's eyes narrowed on me. They swept down to my feet then back up to my face. "Aren't you his resident? Oh, the board will have a field day with this. My God, you two are foolish."

He started to back out of the room, and Ethan reached for him. "Jack, wait..." But Dr. Hayward slipped out and shut the door before Ethan could catch him.

My heart hammered against my ribcage as I watched Ethan scramble to put his shirt and shoes on. I stood there like a statue, paralyzed by the fear of what he was thinking and what might happen.

"Ethan..." I muttered, but he was flustered, mumbling something under his breath about the hospital policy and this being disastrous. My stomach churned, and I thought I might throw up. I picked up my underwear and put them on, then my bra. Ethan was tying his shoes when he let out a growl of frustration.

"I told you we couldn't be doing this." I didn't take it personally because he had as much say in what we did or didn't do. It wasn't like I forced him. He was a willing participant. Besides, I knew he loved me and this moment would pass.

"Babe... Try to take a deep breath." I slid my shirt on and stepped into my pants, but I could see clearly that he was not going to calm down. He was probably as afraid as I was. The policy was very strict and left no room for interpretation. This could lead to one or both of us being terminated if Hayward decided to snitch.

"Take a deep breath? Lily, if Jack goes to HR, we're screwed! Do you understand what that means? One or both of us is getting fired." Ethan ran his hand through his hair frantically as he looked into the mirror hung by the door. "I'm thirty-six with a well-established practice. If I have to get a different job, it means starting over. I'm not starting over at thirty-six."

I saw the scowl on his face in his reflection and felt guilty. If he had gotten dressed as soon as we were done, we'd both have been sitting and chatting. Neither of us would have been naked, but I asked for those precious few minutes of intimacy. Now it was going to cost us.

"Ethan, I'm sorry." I walked over to him barefoot, feeling the cold tile on my toes. It wasn't as cold as the anger in his eyes when he turned to face me. I knew his anger was a secondary emotion, that he was feeling fear and anxiety, maybe even a bit of shame. I touched his face softly, and he grabbed my wrist and lowered my hand.

"Lily, this is serious. I don't know if I'll be able to get us out of this if he goes to the board." His eyes were stormy and dark. They scared me.

"It will be okay, Ethan. We'll get through it. We'll have each other. There isn't anything we can't face. We've had problems before and worked through them." He let go of my hand, but I didn't try to touch him again.

"I have to go. I need to get ahead of this." He pecked me on the cheek, and then he was gone and I was left with my mind swirling. He had never acted this way with me before. I knew it was bad, but it wasn't anything we couldn't handle.

I stood there staring at the open door with my toes curled against the cold floor, fighting back the tears. Even without the overly weepy mood I'd been in, this was a tear-worthy situation, but usually, Ethan was here to comfort me and dry those tears. Now I didn't know what to think. He was really upset. What if he was so upset with me that he ended things? What if it was over?

2

ETHAN

My hands curled into fists at my sides as I stood next to Lily in the elevator on our way up to the fifth floor where the hospital board awaited us. Our Saturday night rendezvous at my place never happened, much to Lily's chagrin. I put it off because I didn't know what to do. I picked up a few extra shifts and worked the whole weekend, and now I was irritable and exhausted, and even the two cups of coffee I'd had couldn't chase away my Monday morning grumpiness.

"Ethan, I really think we should talk." She reached for the emergency stop button, but we didn't have time. She was right. We should have stopped and talked about this, but I knew there was no amount of talking we could do that would make the situation go away. She was needy and emotional, and in my own frustrated state, I'd been burying myself in work to forget about it.

"We don't have time right now." I gently guided her hand away from the buttons, and she huffed out a sigh.

"We haven't even spoken since Dr. Hayward walked in on us." Her eyes searched my face, and I avoided eye contact. Her green eyes were tired, and I could tell she'd been crying a lot this weekend. Probably because I had ignored all of her calls and texts.

"What's there to talk about? One or both of us will be fired. We can talk when we know what the board will decide." We'd both gotten the call yesterday afternoon that this meeting was happening and we were required to attend. News traveled fast here at St. Anne's, and Jack Hayward made sure it went straight to the top. That man had absolutely no sense of compassion.

"You don't want to ask me how I'm feeling?" Lily's pleading tone gutted me, but if I broke down right here and now and started talking about either of our feelings, it would open a huge can of worms for us. They'd read it on our faces when we walked in. It was better that we were slightly at odds right now. It would sell my story to the board much more easily.

"When the meeting is over, okay?" I snapped, not intending to come across as angry with her, but it silenced her clinginess and the elevator came to a stop. The doors slid open, and I led the way toward the board room. Lily lagged behind by a few steps, further selling what I'd be telling the board. I hated that I had disappointed her even a little, but it was better this way. At least one of us could keep our job, and it would probably be me. I could help her, support her as she looked for a new place to finish her residency.

She remained silent as we walked into the board room and stood at the end of the large oval table. The board chair, Allen Knobs, stood and scowled at both of us as he buttoned his coat. The other board members remained seated, and Lily ran a hand through her chestnut hair nervously.

"Dr. Matthews, Dr. Carter, thank you for joining us." Somehow, I got the feeling he wasn't thankful at all. His tone was disapproving and gruff. "As you both know, there have been some serious accusations brought against you by one of your colleagues." I hated the way he looked down his nose at us, like he was better than us and had never made a mistake in his life.

"Yes, sir," Lily mumbled, and I wished she'd just let me do the talking. I glanced at her and glowered, but her tight-lipped expression was focused on Allen.

"We can just make this short and sweet if you want." Allen's forehead was furrowed, deep crevices stretching parallel to his eyebrows. His balding head shone under the fluorescent lights reflecting the white-blue glow. I didn't know what he meant by short and sweet, but it didn't sound good.

"Sir, if you let me explain—"

"Explain? Dr. Matthews, you were found in the doctors' on-call room with Dr. Carter who was in a very inappropriate state of undress, and you yourself were half naked. There is little left for the imagination. I have only one question." Allen's glare locked on my face. "Did you have sex with Dr. Carter Friday evening in the doctors' on-call room?"

He wasn't making it easy for me at all. I had an entire speech planned out to explain how this was a random one-time thing that would never happen again. Of course, that was utter bullshit considering we'd been dating seriously for more than six months with a few months of a fling before that. Lily and I were headed toward a real relationship. We just had to navigate the red tape of hospital policy first.

"Sir, it was a mistake."

I heard Lily suck in a breath and almost audibly scoff, which would only destroy my chance at selling this.

"Dr. Carter and I are only human. We got carried away. It won't happen again—"

"You're damn right it won't happen again." Allen shook his head and continued. "We have rules for a reason, Dr. Matthews, and I don't take kindly to men who think they're above them. What you did is unthinkable. Sex on hospital property while you're on the clock, with a subordinate, no less? Do you realize the egregious misuse of hospital time and resources you're guilty of?"

"Allen, please, I—"

"That's Dr. Knobs. I'll thank you to keep this meeting professional, which is something you seem to have a difficult time doing. Now, I want to know how long this has been going on. Because I can't fathom a man of your stature with your career on the line would make such an obvious mistake." He waited, staring at me, and I had only one response.

"I told you. It was a mistake." I squared my shoulders and awaited my punishment, praying for Lily's sake that it wasn't that bad. There were loopholes in the policy that allowed the board room for leniency, but I didn't think we'd get any, judging by the expression on Allen's face.

"Well, your mistake has cost you." He sat back down and unbuttoned his jacket as he did so. Then he picked up a manilla file folder from the table in front of him and opened it. The thick gray mustache resting on his upper lip twitched as he read from the file. "Dr. Matthews, you are on probation. You will report directly to Dr. Hastings in all matters. She will oversee your practice for the next six months. Your pay will be docked twenty percent for the duration of your probation, and any further infraction will be grounds for termination."

So they weren't going for the jugular, at least not with me. But I knew Lily was vulnerable. Being a resident, she was held to the highest standard. The hospital wouldn't employ doctors who couldn't follow rules, and most of them were weeded out during residency to avoid more problems when they had larger salaries and practices.

"Dr. Carter, you're fired." Allen slid his glasses down the bridge of his nose and looked at Lily over them. I had to force myself not to look, especially when she started crying. "You might think long and hard about your life choices before signing up for a residency anywhere else. What you do in your formative years of medicine follows you the rest of your career. You can't afford to make poor choices like the one you made with Dr. Matthews. You're dismissed— both of you."

Lily turned abruptly and walked out, and I followed on her heels. With her being terminated, we'd be free to pursue our relationship now without the struggle, though I didn't know where she'd get a job now. I wasn't celebrating that, though, because I knew how difficult it would be for her and what this would mean for her career going forward.

When we were back in the hallway, I reached for her hand and she yanked it away. "Don't touch me." Lily sobbed and covered her mouth as she walked right up to a trash can and threw up. It was hard watching her hurt so desperately. I held her hair back for her through the worst of it, and she smacked my hand away when she took a breath. "I said don't touch me."

A nurse pushed her med cart past us and gave me an odd look, but I didn't care. Right now, Lily was the only thing that mattered.

"Listen, I'm here. We can talk now." My chest was tight and my mind was racing. She'd been upset with me before, but never like this. Never upset enough to push me away.

"Talk now? You mean after you called me a mistake?" She straightened and swiped across her face with the sleeve of her lab coat before tearing it off and throwing it in the trash can, covering her vomit.

"Please… Lily, a one-time thing doesn't look as bad to the board. If we'd been honest about—"

"If we'd been honest, I'd have said I was in love with you and that I wanted a family with you. I wouldn't have called you a mistake." She turned and stormed up the hall, and I chased after her.

"Could you please listen to me?" I grabbed her hand, and she spun around and with her other hand, she smacked me hard across the face.

Her entire body shook with anger and emotion. "Was it ever real, Ethan? Did you really mean it when you said you loved me, or was that a mistake too?" The rage in her tone coupled with the pain in her eyes had me speechless. I fumbled for words, uttering unintelligible words until she was in the elevator on her way down to the ground floor.

I stood there staring at the closed elevator doors wondering what the heck just happened. We were so happy last week, so in love. I was going to ask her to move in with me and eventually to be my wife, and now it felt like I was losing her entirely. I pressed the elevator call button furiously, hoping to catch the next box down, but the light stayed lit, the elevator doors shut.

So I ran. Nurses looked at me oddly, and one orderly with a mop bucket cursed at me as I raced past, but I ran to the stairwell and downward. I had to catch her before she left. I didn't want her driving home on icy roads as angry as she was. Denver was a bear in winter, and she wasn't thinking clearly right now.

I'd been a fool. I'd used my own anger at the situation as a barrier between me and my emotions, and Lily had been the one to pay for it. I hated myself for that. But by the time I got down to the ground floor and back to the main entrance, I saw her tail lights as her car pulled out of the parking lot. She was really angry this time. I'd really done it. I stood there watching the red of her taillights fade into the bleakness of a gloomy winter morning, wishing there were a way for me to undo what had been done. I only prayed that when I called her, she would answer.

3

LILY

I hovered over the trash can in my parents' kitchen wishing this nausea would go away. I'd been dealing with it for weeks, knowing in my gut what it meant. I just hadn't had the courage to take the test to confirm it. Though, I had purchased one.

"Honey, you get yourself so worked up." Mom was there, holding my hair up and rubbing my back as my stomach emptied itself for the second time today. I hadn't spoken to Ethan since the board meeting on Monday morning and now, being Thursday afternoon, I still had no intention of returning his calls.

"Tissue," I grunted, and Mom left my side. When she returned, she had the box of tissues from the living room in hand. She pulled a few out and handed them to me, and I blew my nose and wiped my face clean. She was a smart woman. She'd figure it out soon enough, but even still, I couldn't face that thought. If I was pregnant, I was doing it alone, and that hurt. Almost as much as Ethan's words in front of the board.

"I can't believe I'm fired, Mom. I needed that job so badly." I tossed the tissues into the trash and slogged over to the dining room table and sat down. Not even the view of the Rockies out the kitchen's picture window could cheer me up, and I'd been missing this view since I took that residency on the other side of Denver last summer. Despite only being three hours away, it seemed like worlds apart from my parents' place.

"I know, honey, but you'll find something soon." Mom sat with me, carrying her cup of tea, the smell of which was what had triggered the vomiting, not the emotion like Mom thought.

Her warm brown eyes were compassionate as she touched my hand softly and smiled. "You're a brilliant woman, Lilian. Any place would be lucky to have you."

Dad offered to pull some strings and help me get into a good residency here, but I didn't want favors. I wanted to do this on my own, the way all other doctors did. It was bad enough that I was back under their roof at the age of twenty-five. I felt useless and desperate.

"I just can't believe he said I was a mistake." The tears welled up again as I thought of the tone of Ethan's voice when he told the board chairman that. It was a hot knife in my chest that I still couldn't pull out. How could he call me a mistake? After everything we'd done together, the way he told me he loved me and the way we dreamed about a future together. I deserved better than that. I deserved an explanation, but I didn't even want one. It wouldn't matter. It hurt too badly to hear the first time.

"You deserve someone who doesn't have any doubts about you or your future. Someone who will fight for you in difficult situations. Lily, it sounds like maybe this Ethan fellow just isn't the right one for you." She patted my hand then squeezed it, and I felt my stomach knot up again.

Ethan was the perfect man for me. I loved everything about him. We had an ease to the relationship that most people never had. We almost never argued, but when we did, we were able to step back and talk rationally when it was over. We could talk easily for hours about anything. He made me laugh, and I made him happy, or at least I thought I did. Until he called me a mistake.

"Yeah..." I agreed numbly with Mom's words, but up until Friday, I'd have said Ethan was that man who had no doubts about me. Now, I didn't know if I'd ever know when a man was being truthful with me again.

Everything changed the instant Dr. Hayward walked in on us. Ethan had been overly cautious the whole relationship, and I knew why. He told me he was afraid something like this would happen, that one of us would be fired. But now I knew deep down that he was just ashamed of his "mistake". It made me question whether any of the past nine months with him were even real or if he'd just been stringing me along for the amazing sex.

"You're going to find someone who loves you, Lily. And you can stay here until you find the right residency program to get back into the game. And if you find a place here in Denver, you can stay as long as you'd like. No need to feel pressured to move out." Mom's hand withdrew, and she picked up her mug of tea and sipped it as my stomach rolled again.

"I'm sure Kate will love that." Kate, my younger but needier sister, lived across town after a few months of my parents' badgering her to grow up and become more responsible. When they started forcing her to pay rent, she finally decided if she was going to have to pay, she'd rather be on her own. She found her own place and now resented me for being the responsible one who didn't need Mom and Dad. I hadn't heard from her since I got home yesterday, but it was only a matter of time.

"Kate will get over it. You just take your time. Your heart is broken right now." Mom smiled gently at me, and I stood and kissed her on the forehead.

"I'm going to go lie down, I think. Let me know when it's dinner time, and I'll come help cook." I headed toward the guest bedroom where I was staying, and Mom stayed at the kitchen table with her tea.

My heart really was broken. I'd never had a moment in a relationship where I'd become so raw, so disillusioned that I had no interest in speaking to the person again. This one took the cake. Ethan's words cut me to the quick and I was bleeding out now. It made it difficult to even open my laptop and search the job board for a new position. I had no energy, no motivation, just dreaded nausea and so much exhaustion, I could sleep for weeks and not feel better.

My parents' place was small, but the guest bedroom had a private adjoining bathroom. I missed our old home forty miles west of the city, but once Mom retired from being a schoolteacher, Dad moved them closer to his job as a podiatrist in the city to lessen his commute. This dinky two-bedroom ranch was nice, but it wasn't the sprawling craftsman I grew up in. It made me ache for any familiarity from my past because I felt like my footing had been ripped out from under me and I was floundering in an ocean of regret.

I sat on the edge of the bed and kicked off my shoes and my eyes rested on the nightstand, on the small white paper bag that held the pregnancy test I bought yesterday. A baby would have changed every-thing anyway, maybe for better, maybe for worse, but now it didn't matter. Life had already changed for me so drastically in a split second. The upheaval meant job searching and moving to a new loca-tion. And it meant facing the truth, because if I was pregnant, I needed to know before I took a new residency position. My new employer would want to know. And I would need to make sure I had the support.

If I took a residency at UCLA like the one offered to me last year, I would be completely alone raising a baby. I couldn't do that. I needed a support system like Mom and Kate to help me through it all. If I took a residency here in Denver, I could stay with Mom and Dad, and Kate might even help babysit at times. The first step in this new journey would be knowing, though, and that made me anxious.

I picked up the paper sack and folded it open to pull out the test. It wasn't the first pregnancy scare I'd had with Ethan, either. We'd been screwing around at work for about three months when I thought I was pregnant— sore boobs, tired, the works. I took the test, and it turned out I wasn't. My thyroid was underactive and causing some issues. But after being on the proper meds for a few months, that worked itself out. The doctors said it was stress-induced and I agreed with them. Sneaking around was stressful, but I'd learned to manage that stress.

This, however, was different and I knew it. Last time, there was no nausea or excessive crying. I could chalk the tears up to being heart-broken, but that would be a lie. I was overly emotional about things before any of this blew up, and I'd been hiding it from everyone. Professionals don't cry at work.

It was time. I had to know. I took the test into the bathroom and set it on the sink as I pulled down my pants and sat on the toilet. I didn't even bother shutting the door. Mom would never just walk right in here. She thought I was napping, and after this, I'd be crying myself to sleep for sure, anyway.

I tore the box open and then the foil pack that contained the plastic wand. When I peed on it, I made a mess and got it on my hand. Frustrated, I set the test to the side and finished, then washed my hands and returned to see the test was already processing. The results window already showed a faint pink pair of lines that didn't even surprise me. I stood there watching the lines grow darker and darker, and tears welled up.

This should have been a thrilling, happy moment for me and Ethan. I should have been overjoyed at the idea of telling him he'd be a father, that we would have a family. Now, all I could think was that if he thought I was a mistake, what would he call our baby?

I pressed my hand to my lower stomach and blinked out a few tears. My heart was a little fuller knowing I was right, that I'd be a mother. I knew it was stupid and would be crazy difficult, but I wanted it. I wanted to feel my baby moving inside me and kicking. I wanted to give birth and experience the joy of bringing life into the world. And most of all, I wanted to love and be loved in the purest bond I'd ever have. I just wanted it with Ethan by my side, and that would never happen.

I could never tell him about this baby, at least not while my heart was so torn up. Which meant being alone and staying in Denver. It was better this way. If I went back to clear things up and tell him, I'd listen to him apologize and say he was sorry. I'd take him back, and somewhere further down the line, he'd do something worse. Or worse still, he'd just reject me outright because what we had was never real.

I didn't want my baby to grow up feeling like a mistake. I might not have planned this on purpose, but I wanted it, and I would fight to make sure my little one felt loved from the moment he or she took their first breath.

I tossed the test in the trash and turned the light off, then crawled into bed for a nap. We'd have an interesting discussion tonight at the table, and I'd have to explain to my parents why I wasn't telling Ethan about the baby, but my decision was final. Now I just hoped there was a residency here in Denver. If not, I didn't know what to do next.

4

ETHAN

Eleven months later…

"I'm surprised to hear you're leaving St. Anne's. Is there a reason you're not happy there?" The dark-haired man with thick-rimmed glasses pored over my resume. I sat across the small square table in the common area of Mountain View Hospital's HR department for the interview. I'd already prepared an answer for this question, though it wasn't entirely true.

"I'm happy enough with St. Anne's, but I'm looking to make career moves that aren't available there at the current time." The truth was, walking through those halls and sitting in that on-call room one night a week were eating away at me.

When Lily stormed out after being fired, I figured she'd stop by my place to talk, or maybe we'd connect in a phone conversation and she'd give me a chance to apologize for being so cold toward her. I felt awful. I punished myself for days, then got angry with her for weeks when she ghosted me. But when a few months had gone by, all that anger resolved into disbelief and eventually, depression. I didn't want to keep walking the same hallways she and I had walked together when I thought we were happy. I couldn't.

"That's an honest explanation. Well, here at Mountain View, we are

19

growing exponentially every month, with opportunities to advance opening up monthly as well." He looked up at me and slid his thick glasses off his face, folded them and laid them in front of himself, then smiled. "I'd like to offer you the position of chief diagnostic physician. It comes with your own parking space in the employee lot, four weeks of paid time off, full healthcare coverage, and a few other perks. We can discuss salary later this week if you're interested."

It was a satisfying feeling to be invited for such a prominent position. I felt honored and at the same time melancholy. Leaving St. Anne's was the best thing I could do, both because of how it strategically helped my career and because staying meant being bombarded by memories of Lily which distracted me from doing my best work. But it meant leaving behind a part of my heart I knew I'd never get back. I wouldn't get it back if I stayed there either, but part of me still enjoyed the nostalgia of those memories.

I reached across the table and extended my hand, and the man shook it. "I am deeply honored to accept your offer." His grip was firm and decisive. He knew he wasn't making a mistake, but part of me wondered if I might be. Changing things in my life after Lily without closure for that relationship felt like I was betraying her, even though she was the one who left abruptly without any explanation. Eleven months later, and I still knew nothing, only that she was angry and hurt.

"I'm so glad." The man let my hand go and stood. He collected his files and stacked them as I rose with him. "We can get something set up with Tina for later this week. You and I will have some salary negotiations with the board—don't worry, they're very generous. Once I show them your CV, they will open their purse strings liberally. And when that's over, Tina can do your onboarding and make sure you're introduced to your team."

Going from the position of attending physician who dabbled in diagnostics to the chief of diagnostics was a huge step. But it was one for which I was ready. I'd been preparing for years, learning the skills and studying constantly to stay ahead of the medical game. It was a bold move but it had to be done. I couldn't sit around and wallow in self-pity anymore. I had to move forward, even if my heart wasn't ready to move on in a new relationship.

"I'll wait to hear from you, then. It was nice meeting you. I look forward to getting started here at Mountain View." I shook his hand again before exchanging goodbyes, and then I was off. This late in the evening, the gang from St. Anne's would be at the pub for drinks. I was grateful to the team at Mountain View for scheduling this second-round interview later. Despite having already announced my desire to move on, the team at St. Anne's and my patients there still needed me.

I left the hospital and climbed in my car. Now with only two weeks left to work where I was, it meant saying farewell to some of the best coworkers in the world. It also meant answering some tough questions from them. Tonight when I told them I'd be taking the job at Mountain View, it would mean feeling like part of me would be displaced for a while until I found my footing in my new position.

Wrestling with the past and how things went down with Lily wasn't easy, either. My probation had been lifted five months ago, but even with the return to normalcy, it wasn't normal. My lunches were lonely now, my evenings quiet and empty. I fell into a depressive lull in life and even stopped working out. I did pick up a drinking habit I wasn't proud of and a few extra pounds around the middle that I had later worked off by punishing my body through hard exercise.

But nothing would bring her back to me. I had been foolish and thought protecting my career was better than standing up for our love, and it had gone horribly wrong. I had basked in self-loathing so long it had become my new identity, pushing myself to be better and do better, but with this change in jobs, that would change too. I might not start dating again, but I had to get over it and focus on my future. Otherwise, I'd end up dying a lonely hermit who never progressed past general physician.

The lot was full so I had to park on the street. Before I was even in the building, a few nurses joined me on the walk. One of them had been making eyes at me for months now, flirting a little. But I'd been rejecting her advances on account of our being coworkers.

"Hey, Dr. Matthews." Her cheery smile should have smoothed some of my rough edges, but my ambivalence prevailed.

"Uh, hi, Casey." I held the door open as her two friends entered first. She followed them, but she hesitated by the door as if she were waiting on me.

"You seem a bit down. Everything okay?" Her question met me as I stepped into the dim pub. It was packed already, with only a few bar stools available, which I preferred over a table or booth. At least at the bar, you could feign ignorance when someone sat down next to you and you didn't want to talk. It didn't appear it was going to be that easy with her, though. She nearly clung to me as I stalked over and planted myself on an empty stool.

I should have been thrilled, on cloud nine even. The job was a huge promotion, and it would come with a substantial rise in pay too. I'd sought it out because that was what I needed. But I felt less excited about it than I should have been.

"Actually, I just accepted a job offer." I raised my hand in the general direction of the bartender, who was quite busy. He nodded at me, acknowledging he'd seen me, and then he kept filling orders. I didn't need to tell him what I wanted. He knew me too well now. I'd become a regular since Lily left.

There was her name again. Always on the tip of my tongue, in the back of my mind. I wondered when I would ever get over her and let my heart start to forget how incredible I had it before I screwed things up.

Casey wedged herself between my barstool and the one next to me which was occupied by another man. I'd seen him around but didn't know him personally. Casey seemed completely unaware that she might be encroaching on his territory and bothering him.

"New job? Where at?" Her elbow slid across the bar, and she rested her head on the heel of her palm. Soft blonde curls drooped from her head. She was cute, a bit older than Lily, but attractive. Still, I had no interest in her or any other woman. My heart still belonged to Lily even if she didn't want it. I doubted that would change any time soon.

"Mountain View... I'll be the chief diagnostic physician..." The title would have drawn awe from any of my doctor colleagues, but Casey shrugged it off and flipped her hair over her shoulder nonchalantly.

"So you won't be working at St. Anne's? That's sad..." Her bottom lip pouted out, then instantly retreated as she smiled. "That means we won't be coworkers anymore." Her fingers walked up my bicep, and then she traced a line back down to my elbow where she let her hand drape across my exposed skin.

"I guess not..." I replied, and the bartender set my glass of beer in front of me. A few of these and I'd be feeling fine. Not fine enough to forget how badly my heart had been trashed and hook up with Casey, but fine enough.

"Ethan, you and I could finally go on that date. You know I've been waiting around." She flashed a bright smile at me, dazzling baby blue eyes, a dimple on her left cheek. I'd have taken the bait for sure a few years ago. She was smart and gorgeous, but she wasn't Lily. "The non-frat rules won't apply anymore."

I sighed into my beer and took another swig. Letting people down easy wasn't my strong suit. It was the reason I'd found myself attached to Lily in the first place. I cared how people felt and it got me into trouble, but this time, setting a personal boundary was a must. It didn't matter that Lily was gone. I still loved her.

"I'm sorry, Casey." I turned to see the disappointment creeping into her expression as it had done every single time she'd asked me out and I'd said no. "The truth is, I'm still hung up on someone and I'm not sure when I'm going to get over that. You are a beautiful woman and you deserve a man who can give you his full attention. With the new job, I'll be on a learning curve for months with little to no free time. And even in my free time, I'll be thinking of the one who got away."

I expected her to be angry or frustrated with me, but her smile never faded. She squeezed my elbow gently and pressed her lips into a line before saying, "I totally understand." When she leaned in and kissed me on the cheek, it felt like a friendly gesture, not a move of seduction. "Just know that I'm interested and when you feel like you're ready to move on, I hope you'll consider giving me a shot."

It was a very mature response to my rejection, and it made the weight melt off my chest. I nodded at her and brought my beer glass back to my lips. Who'd have thought I'd be the type of man who turned gorgeous women away because I was still in love with someone who clearly didn't want me? But I couldn't drag any part of my life at St. Anne's into my future. If I did, there was no point in moving on at all. Lily would follow me everywhere. Cutting all ties was the only way.

And it hurt like hell...

5

LILY

Four years later....

"Dr. Lilian Elaine Carter!" When the dean of medicine announced my name, I stood and strolled up to the stairs and across the platform. Such pride swelled in my chest at my accomplishments that tears welled up and rolled down my cheeks. I strutted over to receive my official diploma, along with board certification and licensure, and the dean shook my hand firmly.

My family, seated in the massive crowd, cheered loudly and whistled. I turned to face them briefly and spotted Mom clapping wildly with such joy on her face too. A few of my cousins, my Uncle Mike, and even Dad all stood to their feet, cheering. But the face that made my tears gush was Noah's.

His chubby little cheeks were flushed from the heat of the sun overhead, and he rubbed his eyes and then clapped too. Four years old and so full of life and love, I was so glad they allowed him to come to celebrate with me. My son was my everything, and having him here as I finished my course of studies and board exams meant everything to me. I blew him a kiss, and he covered his mouth and smiled. I could almost hear his giggle.

They ushered me off the stage, and I found my spot with my peers.

There were a few more short speeches and a few songs. Then we tossed our caps high into the air in celebration and I was done. My four years of college, a break while I recovered from giving birth, my years of residency, and finally, it was done. I was a full-fledged doctor in my own right, and it felt amazing.

After collecting my cap from the mass of bodies stumbling around, I hugged a few friends whom I knew I might never see again and made my way through the crowd to find my parents. They stood near the far end of the football field, waiting for me. Dad held Noah on his hip, and Noah lay draped over Dad's shoulder almost ready to fall asleep. His nap time coincided with the ceremony, but I insisted they come anyway instead of just babysitting.

"Oh, honey, you did so well. You must be hot under that robe." Mom handed me a bottled water, and I leaned forward to brush a few strands of Noah's hair off his sweaty forehead before Dad turned to peck me on the cheek. His rough stubble scratched my cheek the way it always had my whole life. It was something I could count on.

"Congratulations, baby," Dad said softly. "I'm really proud of you." He didn't even have to say how proud he was. It was written across his aging face. A smile reached his eyes that sparkled with joy.

I cracked open the bottled water and had a sip before responding. "Thank you. How did he do?" I asked, knowing just how challenging my little man could be at times. Graduation ceremonies weren't exactly conducive to small children, but he looked content.

"He had an accident and I missed your speech," Dad told me, "but I got him cleaned up and Mom recorded it, so I can watch it at home. Noah's just tired now. We should go get him out of the sun and get some lunch."

I hooked my arm around Mom's and followed Dad across the stadium to the south exit where Dad and Mom had parked. She was right. The cap and gown were excruciating. The black material had me baking in the bright sunlight, so I shed it the minute we were at the car. I'd taken an Uber to the stadium this morning, so I climbed into their back seat next to Noah's car seat and got him buckled in as Dad got the car started and cooling off.

"You know," Mom said as she climbed in, "Aunt Betty was asking about Noah. She thinks he's too small for his age." Mom's sister was nosy, but she was right. Noah was small for his age. He should have been in a booster at the age of four, but his poor body had been through so much.

"Yes, well you told her preemies are always a little small for their age, even into adulthood, right?" I hadn't told anyone other than my parents about Noah's condition, and I didn't intend to start telling them now. He didn't need a stigma surrounding him. By the time he was in high school, this would all be behind him.

"Yes, dear. I just think—"

"I know, Mom. But I don't want people talking about him. Words are powerful, and I don't want that sort of negativity going through his thoughts as he grows up." I snapped the chest restraint into place as Dad pulled out into traffic, then buckled myself in. Mom grew quiet, dropping her argument, and I settled in for the ride.

We had already decided on eating at a small Mediterranean restaurant after the ceremony, and I thought we'd agreed on not talking about Noah's health, especially after my aunt gossiped about Kate's miscarriage last month. I put it behind me when he was eighteen months and had his first surgery. The trauma of it all still tormented me at times.

"I'm really proud of you, sweetheart," Dad said again, eyeing my reflection in his rearview mirror.

"Thanks, Dad." Being a single mom for the past four years had been challenging. Months in the summer without Noah around, long periods of time where I only saw him for a few hours every day while he was at daycare or babysitters. And I hadn't even been home for Christmas once, though Noah flew back with Mom each year to be with family. It was a break for me, and some Nana and Pop time for him.

"Have you given any thought to your next move? You've gotten some offers, right?" It was his job as a dad to worry about me. I was still a baby to him, though I was actually twenty-eight and well able to care for myself. I knew I'd probably still be worrying about Noah when he was an adult too. It was in a good parent's nature.

"I have..." I responded, but it wasn't as much "thought" as it was worry. I avoided looking at the mirror because I didn't want him to see my uncertainty.

The job at Princeton-Plainsboro would mean a very cushy salary. As chief pediatric attending, I'd have a nice title and be able to afford an upgrade to my stuffy one-bedroom apartment. But it would mean continuing my life as a single mom on my own without the support of my family. Kate had even settled down and gotten married, though lately, her life had been bumpy after miscarrying for the second time. But she promised to babysit if I moved home.

Which brought up the idea of the position as pediatric attending at Mountain View in Denver, only miles from my parents' house. It wasn't the same stature as the job at Princeton, and the salary would be lower, but cost of living was lower too. And I'd be right back in Denver with my parents and Noah would have his Nana and Pop nearby. Plus, he loved Aunt Kiki, which was what he called Kate. I just didn't know if I wanted to be in the same city as Ethan again or risk him seeing me somewhere with Noah and putting the pieces together.

"What do you think?" Dad was prying, and I wanted to tell him to back off, but I knew he cared.

"I don't know. I'm still thinking." I had no other response. Dad would keep asking, but I needed time to decide what I wanted for my future as far as my career went, and my son too. Knowing Ethan was near Denver at St. Anne's only complicated things because I'd kept Noah a secret.

I stared out the window as Mom changed the subject and talked about the traffic. She distracted Dad from his interrogation and I was relieved. She knew how hard this decision had been for me, and now I only had a week left to decide what I'd do. It kept me up at night obsessing over the tiniest details.

At lunch, Dad sat across from me where he could look me in the eye, and Mom sat next to him. Noah sat in a booster next to me in the small booth with its red leather seats. They chatted about the menu, and I pointed out the images of food on the children's menu to Noah, who scrunched his nose and pushed his glasses up with a finger, leaving a smudge on the lens.

"Look, buddy, what do you want to eat? They have chicken fingers, and mashed potatoes. Or you can get pizza, or how about grilled cheese with apple slices?" Each image showed an appetizing plate of food, but Noah was stubborn. Getting him to eat had been challenging since birth when his condition was diagnosed. And after his surgery, he barely ate anything for a few months.

"No, I don't like them." He crossed his arms over his chest and revealed his stubborn streak. "I want mac and cheese."

I sighed and again pointed at the other options. "Bud, they don't have mac and cheese here. But I can get you pizza. You like pizza."

"You like pizza," he said, cocking his head. He'd been frustrated with me for weeks. My licensing and board exams had taken almost all of my time, and Mom had been staying with us just to care for him lately.

"Noah, please choose one meal. When we get home, you can have macaroni if you're still hungry," Mom chimed in, and it bothered me that my son respected her more than me. The pediatrician told me things like this happened because children needed a lot of time and attention from caregivers. He'd grow out of it now that I was able to be home with him every night, but it just told me that he really did need his Nana and Pop around.

"I want chicken," he said, sulking, and I was just glad he'd chosen something even if it meant he was responding to his grandmother better than me. I rubbed his back and watched him reach for the crayons to color on the back side of the children's menu.

Not only had his health been an issue, but he had slight delays in physical development and cognitive development too. All of it amounted to a heap of stress for me while I was juggling my residency and trying to make ends meet. I was never more glad to be done with that phase of life.

"You should consider the job at Mountain View, dear." This time, it was Mom who spoke up. I knew she agreed with Dad on most things, and that didn't bother me at all. But their pressuring was without knowledge. Yes, they knew Ethan worked just outside of Denver and that he was Noah's father, but they didn't understand the panic I went through every time I thought of randomly bumping into him. Not only because of the way I left things completely unfinished with no closure, but because if Ethan saw Noah with me, eventually, he'd put the pieces together.

"Guys, please. It's stressful enough to make this decision without being pressured. I know it's a good position and that it allows me to be closer to you, but I don't know if I'm ready..." I let my words trail off and stared at the menu knowing that now that I'd asked them to back off, they would. The choice would be mine alone, and I'd have to make it on my own.

I looked at Noah coloring and saw him make an expression that reminded me of his father. They didn't happen often, but when they did, they melted my heart. I was still in love with Ethan after all these years. Maybe that was why I didn't want to see him.

I didn't want my heart to break again if he was with someone else.

6

ETHAN

The evening had been on my calendar for a few weeks now. It was the night we welcomed all new interns, residents, fellows, and doctors, whether they'd only just been hired or had been working here less than six months. I stood next to Dr. Jacob Vance, a man I'd gotten to know over the past few years. He took me under his wing when I was hired on this very night—the welcome dinner. We hit it off, and we'd been golfing buddies ever since.

"I heard there are a couple of really talented new hires." Jacob sipped his champagne and eyed the room, and I turned to stand shoulder to shoulder with him. There were several new faces and some that were familiar, though I didn't know the people. When they hosted this event for me, I was surprised to see two nurses I had met at St. Anne's were here that night too, hopping from one hospital to the other like me.

That was a good night for me. I felt the break of letting the past go and embraced the newness of the future here at Mountain View Medical. No one knew my personal reasons for taking the new job except me, and I liked to keep it that way. As far as they knew, becoming chief diagnostic physician was my sole motive for the move and it was a good one. I enjoyed the position more than any previous job I'd held.

"I haven't heard much about any of them. I did hear the pediatric wing scored someone away from Princeton-Plainsboro, though." I nodded at Sandra Duncan, one of the board members who had welcomed me into the Mountain View family with open arms. This place felt like home compared to St. Anne's.

"Yeah, I heard the same. She was supposedly on the dean's list and offered chief of pediatrics right out of her residency, which is unheard of, so she must be highly skilled." Jacob's eyes swept the room again and then he nudged me. "I heard she's a babe too." He winked at me, and I knew it was his way of nudging me toward the dating pool, which for the most part, I'd avoided. I had a few dates that went nowhere, dinner and no follow up after that. But I had little interest in dating. My career really was my focus now.

Jacob was happily married, though, and he insisted that I'd be more well adjusted if I had a woman to come home to every night. What he failed to remember was that we were welcoming new colleagues and the hospital policy for fraternization was strict. Not as strict as the one at St. Anne's, but I wasn't going to make that mistake ever again. If I even decided to start dating again.

"You let me worry about who I find attractive, and stop meddling," I told him, chuckling at how forward he was sometimes.

Sandra waltzed up to us with a drink in hand and a smile on her face. The older woman was dean of medicine and one of the board members. She was kind and funny, but she didn't mess around when it came to running this place. I liked that about her, that she could be firm and friendly in the same act. Jacob reached his hand out to shake hers and she gripped it.

"Gentlemen, thank you for coming. It's nice to see our seasoned doctors still joining us for this event." Sandra's eyes sparkled as she spoke, and she pulled her hand from Jacob's to shake mine, which I accepted.

"Dr. Duncan, thank you for inviting us. I remember how warmly I was accepted at my welcome dinner, and I hope the new hires will appreciate your putting this event together for them." Her grip was as firm as her policy, her smile as warm as her heart.

"I hope so too. Would you like to meet a few of the new doctors? I won't bore you with the interns, except those who'll be joining your departments."

"Of course," I said, glancing at Jacob who agreed with a nod. We followed her through the sea of people mingling and chatting. A few of the nurses here looked up to me, and they acknowledged me as we passed them. But what caught my eye was the backside of a woman whose long, curly hair hung loose and reminded me instantly of Lily. I might not have been in the dating game, but I still had eyes, and that ass was perky and round and I might have drooled.

Sandra was headed right toward the woman too, which made my heart skip a beat just the same way it had when Lily and I were messing around. The familiar rush of excitement and attraction was both encouraging and bitter to me. I didn't want to be attracted to anyone else, even if Lily was long gone.

"That's her," Jacob mumbled, elbowing me in the ribs, and I glanced at him.

"The sandy blonde over there?" I nodded in the direction Sandra was leading us, and Jacob smirked and raised an eyebrow.

"I'm telling you, she's cute." His snickers mingled with the attraction I was already feeling toward the woman without even having seen her face, and I felt my body grow warmer. After years of having no true friends, Jacob probably knew me better than anyone else on this planet, and if he thought I'd be attracted to her, he was probably right.

"Pace yourself," I told him firmly, but at the same time, Sandra touched the woman's shoulder and she started to turn.

My heart stopped. Not like cardiac arrest, but the good kind of heart stopping. Same cute button nose, same dazzling green eyes, though she looked more tired than the last time I saw her.

"Dr. Carter, I'd like to introduce you to a few of our department heads..." Sandra gestured at us as Lily's eyes washed across the room to take us in. I stood merely a yard from her, breathing in the scent of her lilac and lavender perfume—same perfume too—and she smiled politely and professionally. Even when her gaze locked on mine, she didn't break character.

"Oh, hello, gentlemen. I'm Dr. Lily Carter, the new pediatric attending." She reached her hand toward Jacob's first, and I stood there stunned speechless. Lily was here? At Mountain View? And she was finished with her residency and now officially a licensed doctor... My mind reeled for what to say or do as she put her hand out toward me.

"This is Dr. Ethan Matthews. He is the head of our diagnostics department. And this is Dr. Jacob Vance, head of oncology. They should be able to help you settle in and meet the rest of the crew." Sandra was so polite and so oblivious. Lily feigned complete ignorance as she smiled at me with her hand held out, staring at my face.

I was the only one who noticed the way her bottom lip quivered as she worried it between her teeth, waiting on me. I slowly reached toward her and took her hand, which was as firm and strong as Sandra's, but I remained gentle, resisting the urge to bring it to my lips to kiss it. The split second seemed to last a lifetime as I looked at her.

Where had she been? Why hadn't she returned any of my calls? She looked healthy but tired. Had she been taking care of herself? My thoughts focused mostly on the woman standing in front of me more beautiful than she'd ever been, and not on the past where the heartbreak lay. If I went there, this would be very bad for both of us. I buried that dumpster fire a long time ago, but I never forgot her.

"Lily," I said softly, and Sandra flashed a look of confusion before starting back in.

"Well I'll be off. Make yourselves at home here. Dr. Matthews, Dr. Vance, show Dr. Carter around, won't you?" She made a point to say Lily's full surname and title, and I slowly retracted my hand.

I was mesmerized and overwhelmed and Lily now looked uncomfortable. Jacob had a shit-eating grin on his face which I wanted to pound off it, but it all happened so quickly, I barely had time to think.

"Excuse me, fellas. I think I need the ladies' room." Lily started away, and Jacob was already laying it to me.

"Man, I told you. Sexy, right? And smart. She's younger than you, but man, I could see you two to—"

"Enough, Jacob," I growled, and without an explanation, I turned and followed her.

We hadn't seen each other in almost five full years and the spark was still there. I felt it when she touched my hand. I saw it in her eyes, and I believed she felt it too. There were hundreds of hospitals just in this state, thousands across the US, and she gave up a job at Princeton to come here? This had to be fate.

She scurried into the hallway with a hand over her mouth, and I was on her heels, stopping her before she managed to get into the bathroom. I grabbed her by the elbow and guided her around the corner where we were just out of sight, and she stood looking at me with a deer in the headlights expression splattered on her face.

"Lily, my God, it's been almost five years. How are you? Where have you been?" I was breathless, not from the chase, but from her. She stole the air from my lungs and I didn't want it back. I wanted her back.

"Ethan, I..." She moved to sidestep me and walk away, but I moved with her.

"You look amazing. You grew your hair out, and my God, you haven't changed a bit... Was your residency good? I assume it was Princeton-Plainsboro?" My heart craved her, yearning to know every detail I had missed. It was like the puzzle piece I'd been missing for half a decade was finally here and I felt whole again.

My fingers itched to touch her, to tangle in her hair and pull her in for a kiss. But she looked down and away, as if trying to avoid me. She'd been avoiding me for years successfully, and judging by her actions, this came as a shock to her too.

"Thank you," she muttered sheepishly. "But I should go."

"Can we catch up? Maybe have dinner sometime? I miss you so

much." I searched her expression, which was pained. I knew she could never say no to me, at least before I hurt her. I hadn't meant to hurt her. It was the situation that ruined us, not by my choice. I'd resolved myself to the fact that it was over the minute we were walked in on. But now, seeing her again made hope come alive.

"Ethan... I don't know."

"Lily, please. Just one dinner. Just a time to talk, to catch up. We don't have to speak about what happened..." I reached for her hand, but she tucked it against her body then wrung her hands together.

"I can't." Lily looked up at my face and grimaced. Whatever had happened in her life had changed her, strengthened her. It was a good look on her, the personal boundaries, but it was bad for my aching heart which needed to be satisfied. Even if only to have my questions answered.

"No dinner, then drinks... How about going for drinks?" I never heard the group coming because I was so fixated on convincing her to go out with me privately where we could become reacquainted, but Jacob and a few other colleagues rounded the corner and almost bumped into me.

"Hey, guys..." Jacob flashed his cheeky grin at Lily and glanced at me. When I looked back at her, she was collected and had her professional plastic smile on her face. "What's going on?"

"I was just asking Dr. Carter if she would join me for drinks and an introduction to Mountain View." I knew just in saying that, Jacob would get my point. He knew me too well to ever get a lie past him.

"Dr. Fun planning a night at the pub? I'm in." He nudged the man next to him whom I didn't know very well and nodded at Lily. "You coming, Dr. Carter? It's always a good time."

She looked ready to reject the invitation, but Jacob's friend joined in, telling her how all the doctors hung out at the pub down the street from the hospital and that everyone would be going. It only aided my case because the Lily I knew and loved came out. She shrugged and sighed and finally relented.

"Fine, I can come for one drink. Thank you for inviting me." Then she winced and said, "I'll meet you there. I really do have to use the restroom." Then she graciously excused herself and slipped away.

"You owe me," Jacob snickered, and he and his friend walked away.

How on earth was this happening? How was this my life? To run into the only woman in the world whose heart had stolen mine after so many years. Fate was giving me a second chance, and I didn't want to mess it up. Not for anything in the world.

7

LILY

When Ethan and the others brow beat me into coming out with them, I knew it was a bad idea. The welcome dinner was supposed to be a brief thing where I could meet my coworkers and then go home to tuck Noah into bed. He'd had the sniffles lately and hadn't been sleeping well. But Dr. Vance insisted and I never could say no to anyone.

So here I was, pulling up outside the old pub. Like St. Anne's, I hadn't been here since the day Ethan broke my heart and I decided it was time to move on. I put my car in park and stared at the marquee out front, lit to cast a glow on the door beneath it. There would be a lot of people in there I knew. Everyone in the city knew it was the place doctors from all over the city descended upon nightly for their sip of sin and relaxation.

When I phoned Mom to see if she could watch Noah, she even remembered the nights I'd stayed out late and had a few drinks with colleagues. She and Dad encouraged me to stay and enjoy myself. I'd been out of town for so long with no one to watch Noah and no friends to hang out with, this night probably seemed like a golden opportunity to them. But to me, it was anxiety inducing.

Dread weighed me down. I couldn't get out of the car. I thought coming back to Denver would be hard, but I never thought I'd walk into my first day on the job and find myself face to face with him again. When I left, Ethan worked at St. Anne's. I accepted the position at Mountain View under the false assumption that he was still there. The shock still hadn't worn off. I didn't know if it ever would.

All my former friends would be in that bar having drinks. Some of his would be too. I knew he was there. I saw his car parked a block away, besides the fact that he was the one who had invited me. If I bailed on this, he'd know I was avoiding him and though there were a dozen excuses why I was, he wouldn't accept that as defeat and leave me alone. We would be under the same roof every day for the foreseeable future.

It wasn't supposed to happen this way, though. I was supposed to be able to settle in and find a routine. Get a new apartment and build my career. Then one day in the future when the fates aligned, I was supposed to run into him at the grocery or the movies. Not this, not at my workplace, not where I needed to be focused and alert.

Someone tapped on my window, and I jolted. I looked up to see Tina Wexler there with a big smile on her face. She stepped back as I opened the door and climbed out.

"Lily Carter, my God. I didn't think the rumors were true." She wrapped her arms around me, and while I should have been thrilled to see a friendly face again, I was sick to my stomach with dread.

"Yeah..." was all I could muster.

"Well, come inside. The gang will be thrilled to see you." She grabbed my wrist and pulled me away from my car before I could grab my purse. I did manage to lock the car, though, so that was good. She gabbed about how things had changed around St. Anne's the whole walk to the door, but the pub hadn't changed a bit.

The old bartender was still the wrinkly, bald guy we knew and loved. The music blasting from the speakers was still oldies from the seventies, eighties, and nineties, and I spotted three regulars in their normal spots. It felt like home. I smiled at the warm, nostalgic feeling and followed Tina to the bar.

"I'm gonna go use the ladies' room. Get me a margarita," she called over her shoulder. The bartender heard her order and nodded at me, and I raised two fingers to indicate I'd like one too. He smiled a familiar smile like he recognized me, and it only made me feel more at home.

Until Ethan plopped onto the empty stool next to me and his thigh brushed against mine. He smelled good, a new cologne for him. Or maybe it wasn't new and I just hadn't been around long enough to know he'd changed to this one. My heart squeezed. I missed him. I missed his smile and his warmth. But the pain of knowing how abruptly he had dismissed our relationship and called it a mistake never left me. It hovered over me like a dark cloud.

"I'm really glad you came tonight." Even the sound of his voice was both comforting and painful. Emotions I buried years ago began to surface, and most of them weren't good ones. I had never dealt with the anger and pain from that day. I just shoved it into a box in the closet of my mind to remain locked up. But he disarmed me, unlocked the closet, and pulled out my box without permission.

"I, uh..." No words would come. At least not words he wanted to hear. All I could think about was the deathblow he'd struck to our relationship and my heart. I was not a mistake then, and I refused to be his mistake again. But I wanted to melt into him and ask a million questions why I wasn't good enough back then.

"You went to Princeton for your residency?" he asked, then he nodded at the bartender, who set two margaritas in front of me.

"Yeah, it just sort of happened." I was slowly starting to calm down. As long as he didn't bring up St. Anne's or what happened there, I would be good.

"I heard they have a great program, and I heard the city is beautiful." Ethan slid one of the margaritas toward me, and I hugged it with both palms. I didn't even know how I'd pay for it since my purse was in the car, but I picked it up and took a big gulp, anyway.

"Yes, it was good. Uh, they have nice parks too." I'd spent the majority of my time in Princeton working, but when I was off, I was with Noah. We spent a lot of time outdoors from March to October, and then we were hibernating or he was with my parents here in Denver the rest of the time. I didn't miss those days at all.

"So you chose pediatrics? I thought you were on a surgical track." Ethan accepted a beer from the bartender who clearly had taken his order previously. It probably wasn't his first drink, either. I never had the luxury of picking up a drinking habit with a toddler to raise, but Ethan always enjoyed a few drinks after work.

"Yes, well, I had my reasons." One of them being my very sick child who was born with a congenital defect. It made me see the scary side of parenting and I wanted to help other parents not feel the way I did when I got ushered through the system. Thankfully, I was a resident doctor so I knew a lot more than most parents, but it never made the worry any easier. Probably made it worse because I knew just how real the risks were.

"I'm sure..." He paused and sipped his beer, then continued. "St. Anne's got to be too much for me. I transferred here almost four years ago now. I can't believe it's been that long. They offered me the head of diagnostics, and I took it."

Hearing that he was moving up in his career made me happy for him. I knew he never wanted to stay stagnant, going nowhere. I was proud of him for chasing his dreams the way I had. But at the same time, I was drowning in shame and guilt. This man who shot for the stars was achieving everything he wanted, but I knew one of the things he wanted was a family—children. And he had a child. He just didn't know about it.

"Back in the saddle already, Doc?" Tina's cheerful voice interrupted my thoughts just as I was about to excuse myself and run away. She pressed a chaste kiss to Ethan's cheek as she leaned between us to get her drink. "Don't let the admins see you over here cozying up." Her snicker as she walked away with her drink in hand only made me want to run away more.

"People talked about us?" I hissed, then I picked up my drink and downed it and set the glass down. Without another word, I walked back toward the door and didn't even stop to think about the tab. I stepped into the cool night air where I could breathe more easily and walked across the street without looking.

"Lily!" Ethan called, but I marched toward my car, ignoring him.

He caught up to me as I grabbed the handle and I froze when his hand covered mine. His body splayed along the backside of mine as another car whooshed past and pinned me against my vehicle. It wasn't unpleasant, but it wasn't comfortable either.

I turned and faced him, and his chest pressed against mine for a second before he inched backward. "I'm sorry." His eyes searched mine, but the only thing they would find would be fear that he would kiss me or shame that I had a huge secret that would hurt him desperately. "Please, talk to me."

"We have nothing to talk about, Ethan. We are two adults with separate lives. We have great careers and we're happy with our families."

"I'm not happy," he blurted out. "Mom and Dad are getting older. Mom lives with me. Dad's in a home. I'm lonely, and I miss you, and I need you to understand that I know how badly I fucked things up. You were right. I should have fought for what we had and I was afraid." His hand cupped my cheek, and my body warmed under his touch.

The apology was too little, too late. His actions had set into motion a cataclysmic journey I could never undo. I ran away from him thinking my baby—our baby—was nothing more than a mistake to him. I lied and hid it, and now Noah was four years old and it was too late to come clean and hope he forgave me. Even if I could look past his failure, mine was too grievous to even speak of.

"Ethan..." I sighed. I turned my head away, preventing him from seeing into my eyes to know my shame. If he wanted to kiss me, he was out of luck. That honor was reserved for someone I could trust, someone who would see my heart and know I hadn't hidden things on purpose but out of necessity for my heart.

"Lily." Ethan used his thumb to turn my face back toward his. It rested in the center of my chin before brushing over my lips. "I never meant to hurt you. I've spent the past nearly five years trying to become a better man. I failed you. I'm so sorry I did. I love you and I always have. I don't think I'll ever stop."

Tears welled up in my eyes at his heartfelt apology, and I wanted nothing more than to cling to him and sob. I hadn't even thought of dating another person since him. Not because I couldn't but because Noah consumed my life. But even if I had, I didn't think I'd have been able to do it. Like him, I was still tangled up in my feelings. No one would ever be to me what Ethan had been.

"I can't."

"Just say you forgive me, and that's enough. You don't have to come rushing back to me. We can take our time getting reacquainted. We can be friends. But my heart is killing me. Knowing you're back is torture, and it's been all of one hour." His brows furrowed. I could see how much pain he was in. I felt it too, but differently. Mine wasn't just an ache for the familiarity of our love, but shame and heartbreak were compounding it.

"I don't know what I feel."

"Have dinner with me." He leaned into me, and I wanted to cave in.

"Ethan, hospital policy. We can't do that again." My cheeks burned, and I looked away again, licking my lips.

"There's a way, Lily. We'll do it differently this time. I need you."

My lower lip trembled and I blinked out a few tears. If he knew about Noah, he'd never be acting like this. He'd be hurt and angry. He would accuse me of hurting him on purpose and make a scene. I couldn't get back into a relationship with him knowing what was going on and have all that weight on my shoulders.

"Please, Lily."

"I'll think about it," I told him, looking back into his eyes. With a hand on his chest, I gently pushed him backward. "I have to go." I climbed into my car, acutely aware of how my heart was hammering behind my ribs. When I shut the door, he didn't walk away, nor did he when I started the engine.

Only when I turned my wheel and put the car into gear did he back up. I drove away sobbing, hating how my heart still wanted him when I knew it was impossible. I couldn't be with him even if I wanted to. I had this secret to keep, and if it got out, it would destroy him. Not to mention what it would do to Noah and me.

I swiped at my eyes and tried to focus on the road, but a few blocks away, I had to pull off and cry. I still wanted him. It wasn't his apology or the pleading for me to come back. It was my own affection. Time didn't heal anything. That old saying was a lie. I rested my forehead on the steering wheel and cried so hard the windows fogged. I should have told him back then. If I had, things would be very different now.

But I never told him and now I never could. In fact, now I could never have him again. I shouldn't have taken this job. I should have stayed in New Jersey. My heart wasn't ready for all of this again.

8

ETHAN

Monday morning at eight a.m., I was seated across from Howard Kratz in HR with a pen in my hand, ready to fill out the necessary forms. This time, I wasn't taking any chances. The most I'd gotten out of Lily was that she would think about it, but I knew her. I'd wear her down and she'd come back to me, and just thinking about that thrilled me.

"Please explain the nature of your relationship." Howard was a drill sergeant, but he was good at his job. I never had to deal with him much, but I knew a few colleagues who had. They'd had issues with personality conflicts or conflicts of interest, never declaring a relationship. But I trusted that he was a good man and knew hospital policy well. God knows, I went home and studied it all weekend after that dinner Friday night.

"Well, we worked together at St. Anne's. We dated for about nine months there and we didn't follow hospital policy correctly. That led to her very unfortunate termination." I folded my hands together and left nothing out. There was no time for keeping secrets or being sneaky. This time, I was doing things the right way, even if there wouldn't be a "this time".

Howard looked up at me over the rim of his thick glasses and pursed his lips. "Termination?" he asked, brows furrowed. "I need more details, please."

"I was her superior. As a resident, she reported directly to me and we had a sexual relationship while thus employed. It was wrong, and clearly, we were punished. I know Mountain View's policy is different, and that's why I'm here. Before I even ask her out on a date, I want to let you know what's happening so we can follow the rules."

He lifted one eyebrow and his pursed lips flattened. "I appreciate that candor, Dr. Matthews. So you're not yet dating Dr. Carter?"

"No, sir, but we had drinks at the pub Friday evening after the welcome dinner and I would like to ask her out." Making my intentions known to HR felt a little like asking her father for his blessing, but it was worth it if she agreed to give me a second chance.

"Ethan, I'll let you in on a little secret. Most couples who declare their relationship don't end up sticking together. It's not that I'm a naysayer, but this place has a way of dividing couples. You seem like a smart man. Do you think it's wise to date a coworker?" His expression shifted from skepticism to compassion. He probably understood better than anyone else because he was the one who dealt with these sorts of situations.

"She works in pediatrics. I work in diagnostics. We're on different floors, different wings. We probably won't see each other at work at all. It would be like she worked in a different facility altogether. I think the relationship will stand on its own notwithstanding the fact we work in the same hospital." My shoulders were squared and he would never shake my confidence.

Howard pushed a stack of forms across the desk and nodded his head while taking a deep breath. "I believe you could pull it off with that type of confidence." His finger tapped the stack of forms and he said, "These need filled out when you believe the relationship is going somewhere. If there is a change, you can update me via email or by stopping in my office. I really wish you the best of luck."

"Thanks," I said, smiling as I picked up the forms.

With a skip in my step, I breezed out of the HR office and into the hallway. Everything about this situation felt different from before.

The weight of nearly five years of depression had lifted at the sight of her, but I was on cloud nine at the thought of getting her back. I hadn't realized just how deeply losing her had affected me. Now that she was back, I felt reborn.

I stopped by my office to put the forms on my desk and field a few calls, then I headed toward the elevators in the B wing.

I didn't have Lily's number or any way to connect with her, so it made my declaration to HR seem even more premature, but I wasn't ashamed, nor was I going to chicken out. Lily had said she would think about it, and that was my foot in the door and the reason I was headed to see her right now.

Too much time had already passed for me to waste a single second waiting on her to "think about it". I knew she probably got slapped with the shock of seeing me again the way I had, and the reason she left still remained hazy. She was hurt, but why it was so devastating that she couldn't speak to me to end things properly had never been discussed. I wasn't really interested in revisiting those old wounds unless she needed to unload on me—which I'd take patiently. I knew I screwed up.

What I wanted was to move forward from here. Just the idea of having her back had me planning for my future. Mom lived in my spare bedroom now, and I had to take her to visit Dad every weekend and several nights a week. Things would be chaos, and Lily might have to understand that date night could be as simple as sitting in a retirement home while my parents visited. It was a different phase of life for me, but I was willing to do anything to make it work.

When the elevator doors slid open to me on the third floor, I walked out with pep in my step. I hadn't been so happy in years. People who passed by me smiled, probably in response to the dumb grin on my face. I couldn't make it go away and I didn't want to try. Lily made me happy all the way to my core, and I wanted the world to know.

I searched for a few minutes before one of the nurses pointed me in the right direction. Lily was with a patient, so I'd have to wait, but that didn't mean I couldn't observe. The patient's door was cracked, and if I stood just slightly to the left of the door, I could see through the crack to where she was interacting. It was a young boy and his parents.

Lily spoke calmly and with a friendly tone. She made the patient smile and put the parents at ease like it was the simplest thing to do. Any doctor would tell you that it was challenging to bring comfort and reassurance to a patient's family, but she made it look easy. And when she wrapped up and walked into the hallway, I was there to greet her. I fell in step beside her and we walked toward the nurses' station.

"Good morning." I resisted the urge to blurt out everything I'd been doing this morning and settled for her response.

"Morning, Ethan. Can I help you with something?" She was busy scrolling through her patient files on her hospital-issued tablet, and I wanted her to pay attention to me, but I stayed patient.

"Uh, just a short personal visit. I didn't realize you were started on rounds already."

Her eyes flicked up to my face briefly before she began poring over the tablet again. "I have twenty patients to get acquainted with. It's my first real day here."

I myself had only four patients, but not many got all the way to my office. I had a specialty and I was department chair. I had people who worked for me to do my rounds. I had forgotten how big the work-load of an attending physician could be in a hospital this size.

"Yeah, sorry. I guess I just forgot." I stayed in step with her as we walked up the hallway, assumingly to her next patient.

"What do you need?" she asked again, but this time she didn't look up. I was bursting with positive emotion and I didn't want to vomit it all on her. Nor did I want to get carried away with myself, because I really wanted to kiss her and pull her into one of these rooms to have the best makeup sex ever.

Instead, I steadied myself and asked, "Can we speak privately for a second?" And when she stopped, I was surprised.

"Anything you need to say to me, you can say right here." She wasn't impolite or harsh. She was being professional, and I respected that. She always had the ability to turn off the personal side of our relationship and compartmentalize better than I did. That was why we lasted so long and it worked so well. We had to hide it before, but she didn't know we didn't have to hide it now.

I took a deep breath and blew it out with as many nerves as I could dump. "I'd really like to take you to dinner, just the two of us."

Her hair had been pulled up into a ponytail, but the curls still reached toward her ears. Her face was plain, devoid of makeup, and her signature scent wasn't wafting around the air like normal. She probably had a scent-sensitive patient. I missed that lilac and lavender scent. But she was captivating and beautiful.

"No. I don't think it will work out." The polite way she smiled could have cut like a knife, but I wasn't one to give up easily. Of course, she knew that about me.

A smile stretched my lips as I remembered the first real date we went on. We'd already been having sneaky sex in the on-call room and after hours in my parked car, but when we decided to make a go of it, I took her to a little Italian place with privacy curtains.

"Remember our first date?" I asked her, reaching for her hand. She let me remove it from her tablet and hold it as I recounted the details. "You resisted me, but I convinced you to go along with me. You thought it would screw up the dynamic we had going by making things real, but we really hit it off.

"We drank way too much and had to Uber to my place, and I made you come five times that night." I winked at her and watched her face warm to a bright pink. "I think that was the best night of my life, second only to this moment now. Please, say you'll relive that with me?"

Lily seemed nervous, biting her lip, trying to tug her hand from my grasp. But I saw the hint of curiosity and desire in her eyes. She blinked several times, and I could tell she was thinking about it. "You know how beautiful I think you are? And I just want a chance to apologize and at least attempt to make things right. Say you'll come. Just one dinner. If it's too much, I'll back off and give you space."

She audibly whimpered and glanced up the hallway, but her shoulders dropped and her head bobbled. "Fine, one dinner, but I really have to go. I have work to do."

"Great." I again resisted the urge to grab her face in my hands and kiss her. "Friday night, and I'll get you details on where and what time. I'll need your number."

She scowled, but she reached into the breast pocket of her lab coat and pulled out a card. "Here. Now go. I have patients."

I practically skipped all the way back to the elevators. It didn't matter that she looked nervous. She had agreed to dinner and I had her back. Now I just had to do my best groveling and maybe we'd get somewhere. A man could hope...

9

LILY

Noah curled up on my lap. His wheezing cough concerned me, but it wasn't croupy or rattling. Unfortunately, it was the mild, annoying type of cough that could come from something as simple as a common cold or as deadly as his CDH recurring. He'd been born with a hernia of his diaphragm, which was life threatening, and he'd already had surgery to repair it, though the doctors told me it was common to recur until he was an adult.

Every time I bathed him my, heart ached that he'd been born into this world, suffering before he even had a chance to know what good health and vitality meant. It affected everything about him—his ability to eat well, to breathe deeply, to function normally. He was a tad behind on cognitive things, but his physical body kept him from doing everything a four-year-old boy should do.

"You feeling okay, buddy?" I asked him, and he curled into me deeper. He didn't have a fever, but he hadn't eaten dinner, complaining of a tummy ache.

"He's fine, Lily." Mom scooped him off my lap and he clung to her. I was so happy he had such a good relationship with his Nana. It felt safe having Mom and Dad around to help me care for him.

"I can stay home if you want. It's just dinner. I don't really want to go, anyway." I stood and reached for Noah, but Mom turned and shook her head, preventing me from taking him back. She walked across the room and laid him in his toddler bed and covered him up.

"I'll read him a story and he'll be sleeping soon. It isn't like we are ignorant, Lily. We raised you and Kate, and I know how to treat a cold. If I need you, I know your number, and you're right across town." She selected a book off Noah's little bookshelf and used her toe to push a few blocks toward the toy box. His floor was littered with them.

"Yeah, but he has a cough..." I bit my lower lip. "I want to be here."

"You need to be where you're going." Her eyebrows rose at me, and I scowled. I'd told her who I was supposed to be dining with, and she was apprehensive at first. Later, she told me it was a good thing, that Ethan and I needed to talk about the future. I doubted very much that tonight would be the night I came clean about Noah, but I couldn't rule it out.

"Read me story, Nana." Noah reached for her, and I was overruled. Even he wanted her instead of me. My shoulders slumped.

I had agreed to this dinner with Ethan feeling pressured to do so, but he was so happy. How could I say no to him? His eagerness was infectious. I wanted so desperately to find peace in my heart with the past and my future at Mountain View that I was willing to sit through this dinner to hear him out. I knew deep down, though, that the shock of having a child would gut him. He would want nothing to do with me then, so the hope would be short-lived.

Maybe tonight was the night I should tell him. If I ripped the bandage off right away, it would hurt less. And it would prevent my heart from getting carried away or finding its way back to him. He hurt me pretty badly, but I still cared, and it took me a long time to realize I probably always would.

"Fine, but you call me immediately if he gets worse." I hated the idea of leaving Noah when he didn't feel well, but I did trust Mom and her instincts.

I slipped out, but before I even got to the car to start it, I got a text message from Ethan. It said his mother, who now lived with him, was sick too. But he didn't have anyone to care for her while he went out, so he asked me to come to his house. A house where we had shared many memories and intimate encounters. I stared at my phone and tried to decide whether it was a grab on his part. If he was trying to get me to come to his house just to pressure me, I wanted no part of it.

But the honest and caring part of my heart knew Ethan wasn't like that. I knew how difficult it was raising a sick child on my own in New Jersey without any support system. He was taking care of two ailing parents alone, and it put a burden on him he didn't have help carrying. I felt like a horrible person for even thinking that Ethan would lure me into his home to manipulate me. He probably needed a friend.

So I responded with a, "*Sure, I'll be there soon,*" and tossed my phone into the passenger seat as I started the car. Ethan's neighborhood had hardly changed. A few houses had new lights out front and the trees were all a little taller, but the same towering mansions I'd grown accustomed to seeing on this side of the city were all still here in good upkeep. I parked out front and took my phone and keys, locking my purse in my car.

When I knocked, he opened immediately, as if he'd been watching me walk up the sidewalk in the dark. Why he wanted dinner so late was beyond me, but I came ready to eat.

"Lily, you look beautiful," he said in greeting. He kissed me on the cheek softly and shut the door, then gestured across his open concept living-dining room and I saw the candles on the table. Their flames flickered and danced beneath the ceiling fan chandelier above. It smelled like Thai curry and it made my mouth water.

"You didn't have to do all this..." I followed him, marveling at the way he decorated the table. The white tablecloth and candles were a sweet touch, but the food had been set out in serving dishes and not just the boxes and containers they'd come in. He clearly had no time to cook last-minute, but takeout was fine with me.

"I'd do anything for you." He pulled out my chair and waited for me to sit, then pushed my chair in when I was settled with my purse on my lap and my phone next to my plate.

I drooled over the spread, at least four different types of curry and rice. There were sesame noodles, chopped nuts, and a crispy sourdough bread all teasing me. "This looks delicious."

I was already reaching for a serving spoon when he said, "Dig in." He watched me spoon portions onto my plate and then served himself. As I took my first bite, he poured a glass of wine for me, which I didn't know if I'd drink. I had to be sober if Mom called about Noah.

"So, you chose to come back to Denver?" he asked, then took a bite of his curry.

We had to break the ice somehow. Our chat at the bar didn't exactly do that. Id' been too cold and anxious with him. It just felt weird being a perfect stranger with a man whom I'd loved so deeply at one point in my life. He used to know everything about me and be able to read my mood by looking at my expression or the way I was sitting. Now, he didn't know me at all. I had grown up and changed. Having a child with a congenital defect did that to you.

"I did, actually. I wanted to be around my family." I had to bite back the bit about my son needing his grandparents. I couldn't tell him like that. He deserved better.

"How do you like Mountain View so far?"

The conversation shifted away from me and directly to my personal likes, and I wasn't disappointed. I was uncomfortable with direct questions anyway, no matter who it was. We chatted about work life and hospital policy. He was comfortable and lighthearted. He even cracked a few jokes about coworkers and who to avoid, but I was having a good time catching up.

Ethan told me how he left St. Anne's for the step up in his career and never looked back. He was well respected now and enjoyed the seniority of managing a team. The confidence looked good on him, and I found myself feeling as comfortable with him as I ever was. We even found our inside jokes were still inside jokes, and it warmed my heart that the years hadn't tarnished that tidbit of intimacy. I was enjoying myself so much that I got disappointed when I heard a bell ringing and Ethan looked up.

"It's Mom. She needs me. Don't move. I'll be right back." He wiped his mouth with his napkin and dropped it on his chair as he rushed off. I watched him scurry away feeling sort of sad for his having to deal with aging parents before he even had a family. With his dad in a home, there was a chance his parents didn't have long to live. It made me feel ashamed that I'd hidden Noah away from them.

I never considered the implications of Ethan's family and their involvement in Noah's life. I felt like a horrible person. They probably wanted grandchildren, and now they were getting older to the point they felt they'd never have them. I wiped my mouth and laid my napkin over my bowl. I couldn't eat anymore.

Patiently waiting, I left my seat and my purse on it and walked to the portrait of Ethan's parents hung over the mantel. The gas fireplace looked like he never used it. That or it was meticulously cleaned after he did. The furniture looked un-sat-in, which saddened me too. It appeared he was so busy working and taking care of his parents that he didn't have a social life, at least not one where he hosted friends.

I moved on to the bookshelf where scrapbooks of memories were stored, but as I reached for one, he returned. I heard him clear his throat, and I turned with a sheepish expression to see his smile.

"Sorry I had to rush away." He glanced at his scrapbooks, probably put together by his mother before she got sick. "There's one of us..." His words hung in the air as he walked toward me. He reached past me, and I was close enough to touch him. I wanted to. That was the horrible part. I wanted to pretend like I hadn't kept a dark secret from him for so long, like I didn't harbor something that could really hurt him.

"Of us?" I asked, but my question was answered when I looked at the cover. Someone had taken the time to select the perfect image of us and decoupaged it onto the cover of the hardbound book. I was smiling, dressed in a yellow and white sundress with a floppy hat the day we went hiking in the mountains, far away from prying eyes. He had brought a blanket for a picnic, and it was the first day I told him I loved him. Those same feelings welled up in my chest, but I had to tamp them down. Getting lost in nostalgia would be good for no one.

"Want to look?" he asked, but I shied away.

Noah was at home coughing and wheezing, and I was here playing a dangerous game. My heart was already attached again even before we'd done anything. This was the Ethan I knew and loved, the one who swore to climb mountains for me. Not the one who stood before the board and called me a mistake. He had clearly gotten my message and knew how that hurt me, and he was trying so desperately to make up for that and all the lost time, but things were drastically different now.

"Ethan, there's something I need to tell you." The weight on my chest was too much. I couldn't let him get any deeper into this than he already was. He needed to know before it got worse and hurt him worse.

"There's something I need to tell you too, Lily." Ethan put the scrapbook back on the shelf and grabbed me by the wrists. "I really screwed up. You were the love of my life and I should've stood up for you. I want you back, and I want to do things the right way. I've already gone to HR about us, and I want to try again. Give me a second chance."

He was so sincere, his expression so earnest. His eyes pleaded with me to listen and respond and my eyes welled up with tears. I was speechless. The heartfelt apology moved me. I didn't want to hurt him, and I didn't want to ruin whatever this was that was happening. My Ethan was here, and I lost myself.

"God, Ethan, I—"

His lips cut me off as they pressed against mine, gently at first, but then more eagerly. The kiss was searing, sucking away my breath and hypnotizing me in its wake. Ethan's hands moved to my elbows, then my hips as I slowly wrapped my arms around his neck. The kiss intensified too, his tongue searching my mouth, and his teeth nibbling at my lower lip.

"God, I've missed you so badly. I thought it was a dream when you showed up at Mountain View. I couldn't believe my luck." His hands fumbled with my shirt as he started backing me down the hallway toward his room.

"Wait, Ethan..." I protested weakly.

He didn't listen, nor did he stop. Instead, he began to undress me, his lips trailing fire on my neck and down to my collarbone. I couldn't help moaning in pleasure as he placed a fiery kiss between my breasts. I was losing this battle I was so desperate to win. It felt so right to be with him again. All my inhibitions melted away as he peeled my shirt off and dropped it. I wanted him—needed him.

The room was dark, and Ethan didn't bother turning on the lights. We groped our way to the bed, tearing each other's clothing off as if it were the first time we'd ever had sex. But his hands knew my body like the curves on a backroad on the way home. He kneaded my bare breasts, pinching and twisting a nipple until we toppled onto the comforter and his weight crushed me into the mattress.

"God, I don't have a condom," I breathed, clawing at his sides as he wriggled between my thighs.

"I'm clean," he panted, guiding himself to my entrance. "Do you trust me?"

I did. I always had and still do. With a whimper, I closed my eyes and gave myself over to him. His lips closed around mine again, and his right hand gripped me behind the knee, lifting my leg. And then he slid into me, painfully, inch-by-inch, until I was gasping and panting for more.

"This is how it should've been five years ago," he growled out. "I'm so sorry I let you go, that I didn't do more to chase you."

I couldn't reply. Ethan began to move in and out lazily, setting a slow but steady pace. It was torture and ecstasy at the same time as he filled me completely, creating a delicious friction that made my toes curled.

"I love you, Lily," he gasped as he suckled my neck. "I never stopped loving you."

My nails dug into his skin as I arched my back, pressing him deeper inside me. It was like we never parted, the familiarity of it, the intimacy of it. He knew exactly how to pleasure me. He remembered how to tease me and push me toward the edge. Every deep thrust hit my cervix at the right angle, sucking the air from me and leaving me whining for more. And when he pressed a thumb against my swollen nub, I knew it was going to be intense.

"Oh, shit, Ethan," I moaned as I rocked my pelvis against his.

"Come for me, baby." His thrusts sped up, his breathing ragged. "I want to feel it."

The orgasm hit me like a wave, crashing over me with such force that I cried out, my back arched off the bed. Wave after powerful wave of convulsions shook me. My hands clung to him, drawing blood, and he only thrust harder. He hadn't lost a bit of stamina since the last time we were together, and I was already feeling almost spent.

"Wow," I hissed, feeling my body grow heavy and relaxed. The orgasm began to subside, and Ethan slowed, but didn't stop.

"I want you to feel amazing because I want you to remember what we used to be. I want us back, Lily." He cupped my cheek and brushed a thumb over my cheekbone. I looked up into his eyes as he slowly drove into me. His pubic bone brushed over my already sensitive clit and continued to push me toward a second climax. Locking eyes with him only intensified that.

"Ethan, I—God," I moaned, unable to form a coherent sentence. He was right, I should never have left him. It was the biggest mistake of my life. What could our lives have been like if I had just trusted him?

His eyes darkened with need, and it spurred me onward. Faster and faster he moved, until I couldn't think straight. His muscles tensed under my hands, and then I came with a loud moan. My body had never been so on fire for this man, and it pushed away the shame and guilt. He was the one for me. He always had been. I'd been so foolish.

"Shit," he hissed just as my climax was waning. He pulled out, gripping his dick, and blew his load onto my stomach. Strings of hot, sticky cum puddled on my skin, and I whimpered from the lack of him inside me.

Ethan pulled away, reaching for the nightstand. When the bed jostled and he returned, I felt his hand wiping across my stomach. "Sorry about that..." He worked until I was clean, and I felt sleep tugging at my eyelids.

"It's okay. Christ, that was amazing." I had no more than caught my breath when the guilty feeling started to sink back in. I never imagined reconnecting with Ethan would feel so amazing physically and emotionally, and I had this cloud over my conscience now.

"You are amazing. You always have been," he whispered, and I felt his hand cup my cheek again. He kissed me tenderly, but the chime of a bell broke the silence. "Crap... God, I'm sorry. I have to go help Mom again. Don't go anywhere. I will be right back." He lingered for a few seconds with his tongue tracing my lips, but I had to let him go.

He vanished into the darkness, and I heard his belt buckle, then saw the light as he opened the door and then closed it. I couldn't stay, though. If I did, he would convince me to stay all night, and Noah needed me. Besides the fact that the guilt was eating me alive. After an interaction like that, I couldn't blurt out such a harsh truth and ruin things for him. I had to pick a time and place that seemed right and hope he wasn't so angry that he hated me forever.

This had gotten way out of hand faster than I thought it would.

ETHAN

I reluctantly pulled away from Lily and left her sprawled on my bed. I grabbed my pants and shirt and yanked them on hastily as I headed for the door and slipped out. I knew when Mom moved in here that it would be a lot of work, and most nights, it didn't bother me at all, but those nights, I didn't have anyone over. Tonight was the first time since the switch happened and Dad went to the home where I felt emotionally burdened by Mom's presence here.

I walked up the hall barefoot, fixing my shirt so I looked presentable as I headed toward her room. Having my mother live with me hadn't been any issue at all before now. I knew she needed me, and I'd decided to make that sacrifice. She and Dad took care of me all the way through medical school and for a few months after residency when I was looking for my full-time position at St. Anne's. Now it was my turn. I just wished it wouldn't affect my time with Lily.

"Hey, Mom," I said when I walked into her room. She was sitting up after I'd already helped her lie down for the night.

"Oh, Ethan, I'm so clumsy. I dropped my medication and I can't find it. Can you please help me?" She looked down at the carpet beneath her feet and frowned, and I sighed.

"Yes, I can help." I walked over to her and dropped to all fours as

I swept a hand under the edge of her bed. She was used to getting her own medication, but there were nights when her arthritis flared up and I had to open a bottle or, like tonight, she dropped something she needed. She couldn't get down on the floor anymore without help getting back up, so it fell to me to aid her on nights like this.

"I'm so sorry, dear. I didn't mean to interrupt your evening with Lily." That was the good part about having her here and not Dad. She was at least considerate about my time and privacy and felt bad for imposing on me. Dad would have milked it for all it was worth. But his health conditions demanded twenty-four-hour care, which I couldn't provide, and he refused to have nurses come into his home. So he stayed at the retirement village.

"It's okay, Mom. I understand, and so does Lily." I found the pill bottle and picked it up. There was no way she could have gotten it herself, and with it being her blood pressure medication, it was important. I was glad I snuck away to help her. I handed it to her. "Do you need anything else?"

"Nothing in particular. How are things going?" She opened her bottle and fumbled out a pill, and I watched her hand shake with a tremor, something that had been getting worse for a few months. I wanted her to get checked out, but she insisted she was fine.

"Uh, pretty decent, actually." I wasn't going to tell her we'd just had sex, but I thought that classified as "pretty decent". I sat on the edge of her bed while she took out her other medications and swallowed them with a sip of water, one by one. When she was finished, she set the glass down and patted me on the knee.

"Now see, when she left a few years ago, you were so distraught. But I told you that love finds a way, and if she was *The One*, she'd be back."

I had told Mom about Lily, almost every detail of it. She knew the depth of mourning I'd gone through when Lily left, and she knew how excited I was when I found her again. We had dinner together a few nights ago when she was in a good spell, and she encouraged me to go for it. I didn't need that encouragement, but having it was special.

"You did say that." I smiled and laid my hand on hers. "How did you know Dad was the one?"

She chuckled, a dry sound that I hoped wasn't going to turn into a coughing fit. "Oh you just know, kiddo. You just know." She patted my hand and closed her eyes. "I was a waitress and he was just another customer, but every time he came in, I'd get butterflies in my stomach. He was so shy with me, always fumbling his change and making small talk, but one day, he asked me out for a soda, and the rest is history."

"And how did you know you were in love?" I asked, and she must have known how I was feeling. I had spent so long in a state of depression and loneliness. With Lily here, life changed.

"When I realized I couldn't picture my life without him in it. I had always been alone and fine, but when I met your father, everything changed. That's how you'll know, when you can't imagine waking up without him by your side." Mom yawned, and I thought about what she said. I already didn't want to wake up without at least knowing I'd see her at work again. The way she vanished five years ago left me with a bit of PTSD that she'd just up and leave again.

"I'm a bit tired now. Can you let yourself out?"

"Of course." I leaned over and kissed her forehead. "You rest, okay? I'll come by tomorrow with more soup."

"You're a good boy," she mumbled as she lay down. I flipped off the light on her nightstand and walked to the door, pausing to look back. I didn't know how many more talks like that I'd get with her, and I treasured every single one.

As I shut the door quietly behind me and left the room, a smile played on my lips. Love did find a way, just like Mom said. Lily was back in my life, and I wasn't going to let her go again. And I knew, deep down in my bones, that this time, we'd make it work.

With Mom tucked in, I returned to my bedroom hoping to see Lily sleeping peacefully and waiting for me. But the light was on, the bed empty. There was a note scrawled on a sheet of paper on my pillow. I walked over to it and picked it up to read it. My heart simultaneously soared and sank.

Ethan,

I had a great time tonight, but I can't stay here. My own personal respon-sibilities call and I have to go home. I'm sure you understand.

But I would love to do this again sometime. Give your mom my love.

XOXO

Lily

I smiled at the note knowing my gut was right. Lily wasn't just back in Denver. She was on her way back to me. It made me so happy that I tossed and turned for hours just thinking of the future and how things might develop with her. My heart was full, despite my bed being empty, because I knew it was only a matter of time.

Love finds a way…

LILY

My footsteps were heavy as I trudged up the hallway to my next patient's room. Seeing little children suffering made my worry over my own son worse. I had three young boys on my patient list who had terminal conditions, and when I interacted with them, my heart broke. As a mother, I couldn't imagine losing my son, especially so young. It was how I knew I was in the right profession. My passion lined up with my education, and I was helping people. I just wished I could help my son as easily.

Tina, one of the nurses, waved at me as I passed the nurses' station. I knew she wanted me to come over there and talk, but I had to make a few phone calls that wouldn't wait. She probably just wanted to gossip about the good-looking male nurse they just hired, or maybe she'd ask me to hang out with the gang after work, but my calls had to come first.

I stepped around the corner and pulled my phone out. I wasn't supposed to be making personal calls during work hours, but when a doctor has a sick child and works first shift, there isn't much to be done. I dialed Noah's new pediatrician's number and waited as it rang through. All of his files from Princeton had been transferred over, and

I had already met with the man once. He was nice and very laid back, though he was nothing like the pediatrician out east.

"Dr. Butler's office."

"Uh, hi, this is Lily Carter, Noah's mom..." I paused, giving her time to look us up in the system. "I just wanted to chat with Dr. Butler about Noah's condition and see what he thought about a few symptoms Noah's having." Biting my lip, I waited as she typed. I could hear her fingers clicking on the keyboard, and then she sighed softly.

"Dr. Butler is pretty swamped, but I think I can squeeze in a few minutes for you. Are his symptoms life threatening or is this an emergency?" The receptionist was just doing her job, but I was mildly frustrated that she would think I would call her if it were an emergency. Surely, she'd read the chart that I was a practicing pediatrician myself. I knew the risks of this condition, which was why I took it seriously.

I'd never treated a child with this particular defect, but I'd heard of it. And I'd been caring for Noah who'd been living with it since birth. By now, I felt like an expert, though I was legally not allowed to treat him, being my son.

"No it's not life-threatening." I tried not to sound cold or irritated. Their ignorance was to be expected. Noah's doctor in Princeton knew us so well he actually consulted with me a few times on his patients later on in my residency. I believed that was because he thought I'd learn as much from the interaction as much as any benefit I might provide him. This new doctor only knew us by the charts.

"Hold, please," she said, and the line clicked over to some cheesy instrumental version of a popular hit song.

I glanced around to make sure no one was watching me while I waited. Getting busted for personal cell phone use in my first few weeks of work wouldn't be good. I was banking on a raise when my ninety-day probationary period was over. Luckily for me, the hallway was mostly dead and Dr. Butler didn't take very long.

"Ms. Carter, how are you doing? How is Noah?" He was such a friendly man. His greeting washed away my frustration instantly.

"Hi, Dr. Butler. I'm doing great. Noah, not so much. I'd like your opinion. Have you had a chance to review all of his charts and imaging he's had done over the years?" Understanding Noah's condition was vital to being able to give me good advice. I knew what I thought should happen, but I didn't want to jump to any unnecessary conclusions. I also didn't want to be too passive if things needed to be addressed.

"I have. Noah is a very strong little boy. So, tell me, what seems to be wrong right now?"

It encouraged me that he'd taken time to acquaint himself with Noah's condition and charts. Noah had a fear of doctors and at times when I wore my lab coat home on accident, it triggered crying fits or nightmares. He had been through so much and at such a young age.

"He's been wheezing and coughing a little. He complains that his belly hurts and sometimes refuses to eat." I knew most of those symptoms just sounded like a four-year-old trying to get out of eating dinner or having a mild cold, but to someone knowledgeable about congenital diaphragmatic hernias, it was a red flag.

"I see, and has he been vomiting? Any fevers, change in activity level or heart rate?" Dr. Butler sounded mildly concerned but not overly. I started second-guessing my own deep worry.

"Uh, well, no. No fever or vomiting. He's just an active four-year-old boy. As far as I know, his heart rate has been normal, at least every time I've checked it. I'm concerned the hernia is returning along the repair scar." I'd seen first-hand how his organs pushed up through that hernia into his chest cavity and caused not only difficulty breathing but pressure on his heart and his intestines so that he wasn't digesting or absorbing food the right way. He was already underweight and below average height for his age.

"I see..." Dr. Butler said something to someone on his end while muffling the receiver, then returned to me. "I'd like to do some new imaging on him if possible. A new CT and an MRI if the CT is inconclusive. How does Noah do with those procedures?" It was so thoughtful that he cared about something like that. I knew I was in good hands.

"He does okay with the tests, just not the white coats. If we could do this at a lab somewhere and not a hospital, that would be best." My thought was double-sided. If I brought Noah here to Mountain View for the tests, Ethan would definitely find out. And if that happened, there would be questions I didn't want to answer. And it would help Noah too. At the lab, they were less likely to be all wearing white lab coats or more willing to break protocol and take them off in order to keep a child calm.

"I'll order them to go to LabTech on the north side of the city. I'll send the orders to your email we have on file too. Let's just have Noah resting more until we get the results. With the lab running them, it could take two weeks. Have him hydrate well, and no romping."

I chuckled until I realized he was serious. "A four-year-old not romp?" I asked. "Do you have children?"

"Unfortunately, no, but I do appreciate the sincerity behind that. If Noah's hernia is recurring, he may need surgery, and if he romps around and tears something, it will only be worse. I'm sorry. I know that's frustrating. Let's run the test, and I'll order blood work too. If things get worse, call me back and of course, I'll leave it to your discretion to take him to an ER if you're fearful."

"Of course, Dr. Butler. Thank you."

We ended the call with pleasantries but no real answers. I knew he wouldn't have any answers for me, and while my gut told me this was what he was going to do, my heart was discouraged. I hated that my son had to go through all this. Maybe I felt a little sorry for myself that I had to carry the weight of it all too.

Then I thought of Ethan and how he was caring for aging parents. My son could have a corrective surgery and grow strong and healthy. With only a few more surgeries before he was in his adult body and no longer at risk of major recurrence, he had his whole life ahead of him. Ethan's parents didn't. They were ailing and aging. Death was right around the corner for both of them, and he had no one when that happened.

It made me again feel so guilty that I hadn't told him about Noah. Ethan and his parents all deserved to know my little boy existed as part of their world. I was ashamed of how I'd handled things, especially after Ethan had been so amazing with me and welcomed me back with open arms. I hurt him, but he loved me anyway.

"Hey, Lily, a bunch of us are going out after work." Tina's voice broke through my thoughts, and I pocketed my phone and looked up at her. She was pushing her medicine cart down the hall. "Want to join us?"

My mind went to Noah and how he'd been a little moody with me the past few days. He liked Nana and Pop, but I knew he missed me after the few weeks I spent unemployed between finishing residency and taking this job. I wanted to be with him too, because if his symptoms got worse, I wanted to be able to act immediately. I couldn't do that if I wasn't watching him.

"Uh, I don't know." I shook my head and held up a hand, and Tina smirked.

"I heard you and Dr. Matthews hit it off." She winked and leaned in. "Maybe he'll be there tonight too."

My cheeks warmed. "Well, we're friends. We go way back to my first year of residency. But I really shouldn't. My son hasn't been feeling well lately. He needs me to—"

"Come on. Just one drink. Show the gang you're not a prude. I'll drive you home myself if you don't have fun." Tina was practically pleading with me, and it felt nice to have people who wanted to hang out with me.

"Alright, one drink, but then I really do have to go home. My son really is not feeling well." I sighed and smiled. I could spare twenty minutes for some socialization. God knows, I needed friends around me when times got tough.

"Yay! See you after work!"

Tina walked away, and I leaned against the wall. Part of me hoped Ethan really was there. I meant what I told him when I left that note. I would like to see him again. Maybe then, I'd have the guts to tell him about Noah. Maybe not, but in the event the topic arose, I had to. I couldn't keep carrying the guilt of this secret. It was crushing.

1 2

ETHAN

I strolled into the pub a little later than normal for a Wednesday. I had a few patients to follow up with for release today before I could leave. I knew Lily was coming because Tina and Amber, both nurses on the pediatric floor, told me. They weren't spying for me, but I might have told them I'd like her to come out more often and given them a little financial incentive to befriend Lily and get her more active in the after-work crowd.

Jacob was here, but I hadn't come to see him. My goal was to get down to brass tacks with Lily. I was so consumed with thoughts of her that it made focusing on work difficult. I'd pretty much withdrawn from any social contact with my work friends because I was so obsessed with rekindling our love.

Lily was seated at the end of the bar alone, and I felt bad. Tina and Amber both had solid relationships with other doctors and staff from Mountain View, and that left Lily alone. She probably felt uncomfortable just approaching them, and they only invited her at my behest, which left Lily to fend for herself. She had an empty glass in front of her, and I was surprised that none of the younger single male doctors were seated next to her. I headed her way.

The closer I got, the more I could see how agitated she was. Her face was screwed up into a scowl. She was staring at her phone and her thumbs were typing in a message that looked heated or flustered. I couldn't tell which. I pulled the stool out and sat down beside her, and she didn't even look up. The message was to her mother. I noticed it as I leaned over her shoulder.

"Whatever you have on tap," I told the bartender, and then Lily looked up.

"Uh, Ethan...." She put her phone in her purse and slid off the stool. "I have to go." The crowd was rowdy this evening, a little louder than normal with the jukebox playing a hard rock song that made it even more challenging.

"What?" I asked, trying to lean closer, but she shook her head. she looked afraid or angry. It was hard to decide which. She scowled and started walking away, and the man next to me elbowed me. When I saw his gleeful expression over my rejection, it irritated me.

I planted my feet on the floor and went after her, finally catching up a few feet from the door. She was in a hurry for some reason, and for whatever reason, it seemed like it had to do with me. She bolted the instant I got here. But I thought our dinner last week had gone so well. She left that note saying she'd like to do it again, but now she was running away and all I did was sit beside her.

"Hey, what's going on?" I asked her, spinning her around. The same deep crevices in her forehead revealed an emotion she was trying to hide from me. She couldn't hide things from me. We'd been together long enough that I knew when she was lying.

"I have to go, Ethan," she said, but I wasn't letting her go without an explanation. I wanted to spend time with her, and I had gotten those nurses to get her to this bar because when I asked her to come she had "other plans". But she clearly had no other plans. If so, she'd have told them no also.

"What's so important?" I wasn't being overly pushy. I let the concern in my tone show, and when the music faded out at the end of the song, it was easier to hear her.

"It's not really something I want to talk about right now." Her eyes were shifty, darting to look at the door, then my face. She wrung her hands and acted flustered. She could tell me anything, but I didn't think she understood that or felt as safe as she once had.

Maybe it had been too long, or maybe she didn't trust me after what had happened. My apology was real, and I believed she had accepted it, but I could appreciate the fact that heartbreak couldn't be fixed with "I'm sorry." It took a lot of time and patience to rebuild trust and intimacy. I was willing to do the work, I just wanted her to stop pulling back. We only just got started again.

"Please talk to me." I raised my hand and cupped her cheek, and she bit her lower lip. Tears brimmed in her eyes, which further confused me. It was something deeply emotional to her, something that touched her heart. I wanted into that spot, but I knew I couldn't force my way in. She had to invite me in, and it didn't appear she wanted to do that yet. I brushed my thumb over her cheekbone as I cupped her cheek.

"Stop, please." She huffed and shied away from me, backing up a step. "It's not really something I can talk about right now. I just have to go. It's important." Lily backed up another step, and I pursued her. She was almost to the wall next to the little coat rack area where we hung our coats in winter.

"Okay, that's alright, but can it wait just a little bit? I wanted to share a drink with you. I thought we'd get some time. Tina and Amber—"

"You put them up to this? Asked them to invite me because I told you no?" Anger flashed in her eyes, then she scoffed. "I should have known. You can't take no for an answer."

My own temper started to rise, swelling in my chest. She had a way of making me feel insanely angry and irrational, but completely in love and devoted all at once. That sort of passion was the type I lived for, where we could throw down like professional boxers and then hug it out and tumble into bed for incredible makeup sex afterward. I didn't want anything less, and I didn't want anyone else.

"I can take no for an answer. I just prefer an explanation with it." I moved forward again, and she bumped into the wall. Her eyes widened and her nostrils flared. The curls framing her face bounced as she shook her head in disbelief. We hadn't gone at it like this in years, but that didn't stop me from pursuing her. In the past, it always led to the steamiest sex, though that would be a longshot, given we were in public.

"Dr. Matthews, I would politely request you to back up. I do not have to explain myself to you or anyone else. My personal life is my business, not yours." She was so cute when she got angry. She'd get so flustered her cheeks would burn red and her lips would quiver. The tears dried up, and I felt her maneuver her purse between our bodies while my eyes were locked on her face.

"Dr. Carter, I'd politely request you to stop pushing me away when you told me you were pleased with me the other night and wanted to enjoy my presence again." I leaned hard on her, pinning her to the wall and boxing her in with an arm on either side of her. I was getting worked up just thinking of kissing her.

"Ethan," she whimpered, and I knew this time was different. Something was really wrong, but I was carried away. I thought if I just kissed her, calmed her down, she'd melt in my arms and tell me what was wrong. We'd done that too, a few times. I just had to have enough discernment to know what she was feeling. I could see the pain in her eyes.

"Lily," I mumbled, but the train had left the station. I leaned in and kissed her, not as hard as I would have liked to, but she was vulnerable and I wasn't going to push her any further. The kiss was hot, sizzling my mouth, and I knew she felt it too. She was hesitant at first, then leaned into it and let me search her mouth with my tongue.

I groped her, but not too heavily. We were in public, after all, but my dick did start to swell. Just like the good old days, I felt her caving to me, desiring me, until the idiots at the bar made a mockery of our connection and started laughing. I paused and pressed my forehead to hers because it just wasn't working. She was stiff and I was too needy, too hungry for her.

She sighed against my mouth and turned her head. "I'm sorry," I whispered into her ear. "I thought...." My pursuit of her had been misguided at best, damaging at worst. But she knew me. It wasn't like

I had changed in the past five years. I didn't know if I would ever change, but maybe she had.

Lily looked down and away as I gave her a few inches of space. Our bickering seemed to have gotten the attention of a few nearby patrons of the bar. They chuckled and threw jibes at me, and she looked up, horrified. The shame in her eyes was nothing short of gut-wrenching. I hated that she felt that way, that I had made her feel that way on top of what was already happening that made her worked up. I'd do anything to take that back.

Her body tensed, and as I took a step back to turn and tell the bozos off, she recoiled. Her arm drew back and her hand flew toward my face, connecting in a smack so hard spit flew from my lip. My hand touched the spot on my cheek that stung. I was shocked and dazed for a second as she rushed out. The guys at the bar laughed harder, but I didn't have time to waste on them.

I rushed out into the night to follow her, but her car was parked less than three spots from the door and she was already halfway there. Running would only frighten her so I called, "Lily, please. I'm sorry. You can tell me what it is." But before I had my comment out, she was in her car and it was started. She was running away from me and I couldn't stop her, and I didn't even know why she was running.

I watched her tail lights flicker to life and the car vanish into traffic, and I stood there feeling like a total ass. I was selfish and stupid, and I read the situation wrong. She wasn't ready for us to jump back into what we had before, and she wasn't ready to be transparent with me, either. Something was bothering her, and she was hiding it from me. Whatever it was, it was so close to her heart, she had forgotten our dynamic and the way we worked so well together. She'd forgotten how I could help her feel steady in the storms.

I slunk back into the bar and sat on my stool. My drink was there for me, but I didn't even want it. Tina and Amber swung by my seat to say hello and accept their incentive for helping me get Lily to come tonight—a drink each—and a few other doctors said hello, but my mood was ruined for the evening. I paid the bartender around nine and went home to sulk where I polished off the second half of an old bottle of bourbon, Lily's favorite, before passing out in bed to dream of her.

I was off to a crappy start for this second chance. I needed to stop and reassess my game now. If Lily had changed that much, I needed to change too. And I needed to know why she felt like she couldn't open up to me. Because I feared what she was hiding was something she didn't ever want me to know. Was she dating someone else? Or was it worse? Was she just too shy to tell me she wanted nothing to do with me anymore?

My night was riddled with dreams of her, sex dreams and then nightmares of her being torn away from me. I dreamed of her telling me she was in love with someone else, and I dreamed of her saying she was so hurt by my past actions that she never wanted to speak to me again.

But the hardest dream was the one where she lay in my arms sweetly, confessing her love. I woke up around three in the morning to piss, and that was what I woke up to. The dream was so real, I could have sworn she was in my bed, and it was heart wrenching to find the mattress cold and myself alone.

Lily Carter was the only woman for me. I knew it in my heart after years of soul searching and trying to decide what I wanted in life. My attempt to woo her was flawed, and I failed tonight, but I would try again. What else could I do? I wasn't whole without her.

13

LILY

My shoulders were tense and my stomach raw. For three very torturous days, I'd listened to Noah wheezing nonstop. I took a day off work to watch how Mom interacted with him and make sure she could handle his rowdiness, but even in his play time, he was stunted. The lower activity level was an obvious sign that something was wrong. I knew in my heart that the hernia was recurring and he would need another risky surgery, and I was scared stiff.

He sat on my lap in the waiting room with Mom to my right and Dad to my left. The nurse would come to call us back any second for his appointment. We'd rushed the CT and MRI through and today was results day. I was doubly nervous, too. Not only were we going to find out if this was the CDH returning which would require surgery, but we were only one floor away from where Ethan worked every single day. Dr. Butler insisted on seeing us here, and with the stakes so high, I couldn't really refuse. I needed these results.

"It's going to be fine, dear. You know yourself that Dr. Butler is the best pediatrician in the city. We have the best specialists here, and he's been through this once before." Mom's words were an attempt to encourage me, but no sane mother would walk into an appointment like this without some sort of uneasiness or concern.

Being that I had the medical knowledge to know all the risks and exactly how bad it could be for my little boy, I had more nerves than most. I couldn't shut off my doctor brain in this situation any more than I could shut off my mom brain when I was treating patients as young as Noah. My heart was tangled up and overwhelmed, and I wanted it all to be over. Besides the fact that the guilt I now lived under knowing Ethan's parents were aging and probably wanting grandchildren didn't help.

"Dr. Carter..." I looked up to see the nurse standing with her clipboard in hand and a soft smile on her face. I had already asked Mom and Dad to wait for me here. I loved that they wanted to be involved, but this was something I needed to do on my own. I didn't want their worries or questions to make me forget anything I needed to ask or learn.

"Let's go, Noah," I said, setting him on the floor. He seemed so tiny to me now, like a baby, not the four-year-old toddler he was.

He looked up at the nurse with doe eyes and clung to my leg. Someone must have told them he was afraid. No one I'd seen today so far had lab coats on, which was a relief, but he still seemed to know where we were.

"It's okay, buddy." Dad nudged him, and he whimpered, so I picked him up.

"I'll be back..." Mom patted my shoulder as I walked toward the door and followed the nurse into the long hallway. She led us to an exam room near the back with a large television screen doubling as the computer monitor. Noah's CT and MRI results were there, and I didn't need a radiologist to read them and give me the results. I was trained to do it myself.

The large mass inside his chest cavity, which was causing him to wheeze and be unable to take a deep breath, was his stomach and part of his large intestine. The hernia allowed his lower organs to push up through his diaphragm, causing him discomfort and constricting his lungs and heart. It wasn't good at all.

I sat him on the exam table and stayed by his side with an arm around his waist while the nurse took his temperature and blood pressure. Her slight scowl at the blood pressure reading wasn't encouraging, either.

"Dr. Butler will be here in just a second, Noah. We know how difficult it is for him, Lily, and we're going to make this as quick as possible." She smiled warmly and ducked out. I thought we'd be waiting a few minutes, but Dr. Butler walked right in as she left and he shut the door. He sat on his stool and flopped his file open on the counter.

"Well, Dr. Carter, I'm not surprised given the symptoms you indicated he was having. I'm glad we got the CT done when we did. It obviously shows his hernia has returned. The diaphragm is having a hard time growing with his body as he matures due to the scar tissue. He will eventually need surgery again and—"

"Eventually?" I asked, now clinging to Noah as if he might fall off the table at any moment. I was definitely more scared than him at this point. Eventually didn't sound like the right diagnosis. Noah's body was clearly struggling, and even though I didn't want him to have to endure surgery, I felt it was necessary soon, not *eventually*.

"Yes, eventually." Dr. Butler turned and grabbed a remote off the counter and pointed it at the screen. He pushed a few buttons, and a more detailed view came on the screen. "You see, his heart is struggling a little to keep up with the demands his body is placing on it. His pulse rate is a little too high, and his blood pressure is high too. We need to control these two things well before I would consider him safe for surgery." He turned to me, and I scowled. "He has to be able to handle the anesthesia and wake up."

As a good doctor, I would definitely agree, but as a mother, I worried that the condition would only worsen and start to bring him pain or worse, stop his breathing. Medications could control the issues that Noah was having, but nothing would stop the hernia from getting worse except to sew it shut.

"So, how high is his blood pressure?" I asked. None of this made me happy at all. I didn't want to be here, and being alone made it worse. I should have told Ethan. He should be here to help me make these decisions. As a surgeon and a diagnostic physician, he knew far more than I did. Besides, he was Noah's father.

"Not horrible, but not normal. It's running 130/90. For a child this young, it's dangerous long term, but controllable. I say we put him on some beta blockers to help the heart and the blood pressure, then we recheck in a few weeks' time, see how he's faring." Dr. Butler was a good doctor, and I trusted him. I just wished we could do something sooner. Every minute the hernia was present was a minute he was at risk for lung collapse or even an obstructed bowel. He already wasn't eating well.

"You're sure we can't move faster?" I knew the answer before I asked the question. I just couldn't give up hope that this would be more like ripping off a bandage and less like finding a needle in a haystack.

"I'm sure, Lily. We have to do this the right way or we risk worse things happening. Okay?" Dr. Butler tried to smile at me, but I was too discouraged to return it. "Let's get him on some medications and monitor him. Keep his activity level down, and in two weeks, we'll see how the meds are working. If the BP is controlled, we'll schedule surgery."

I reluctantly accepted his advice and the prescriptions and returned to my parents in the waiting room. They listened anxiously as I gave them Dr. Butler's advice, and they tried to comfort me. Noah, on the other hand, had sailed through this appointment without fear. Thanks to Dr. Butler's staff and their kindness to shed the white coats, he never even cried. I was proud of him and promised him ice cream for dessert tonight if he took a good nap for Nana.

With Mom and Dad escorting Noah toward the elevator, I turned and headed up the hallway toward my office to get my tablet and return to my day's work. I no more than heard the elevator door ding when Ethan rounded the corner from the opposite direction and almost bumped into me. He apologized, and I nervously glanced at the elevators to see the doors closing on Mom, Dad, and Noah.

"Uh, hey..." I mumbled, turning back to him. "What's up?"

Ethan looked at the elevator suspiciously, but my guilty little secret was gone, hidden from his eyes now. "I just stopped down here to see if you wanted to meet me for dinner somewhere..." His eyes searched my expression, but after that incident at the bar last week, I knew I couldn't just open up and tell him. He'd called, but I never answered. He'd texted, but I gave him stunted replies.

My focus had to be on getting Noah healthy first. It wouldn't be good for him or me if I divulged the secret now in the middle of this mess. Ethan had to wait until after Noah's surgery, even if that meant a few months. Even if it meant I lost him.

"I can't," I blurted out, but he wasn't taking no for an answer. He took me by the elbow and pulled me into an empty patient room and shut the door. When he pulled the curtain around us so we were hidden from the view of the window, I knew I was in trouble.

"What's going on with you? We had such a great time. You left a note saying you wanted to do it again, and now every time I make an attempt to reach out to you, you shut me down." He didn't sound angry, but he did sound tense. I wanted more than anything to unload my fear and tell him what was going on, but I couldn't. Not now. I couldn't have a war with him while I was trying to support my son.

"I can't talk about it. I need space," I blurted out, and I was afraid. What if he'd seen Noah? What if he was asking different questions? This was hitting too close to home too quickly, and I felt panic rising. I tried to step around him, but he hooked an arm around my stomach and I snapped. "Stop it. Just stop trying to control me."

"Hey, whoa. I love you, Lily." Ethan tried to calm me, but I was inconsolable. I knew if he saw Noah, things would be ten times worse.

"Love me? Why didn't you stand up for me five years ago, then?" I let the words come barreling out of my mouth, but I didn't mean them. Though I'd never gotten the chance to really confront him, I accepted his genuine apology the other day and I meant it. I just had no other reason to explain why I felt so cagey.

"Lily, what's going on? What happened?" He didn't understand and he wouldn't. I just needed to get away from him and cry. Getting the news from Dr. Butler was bad enough, but this was only adding insult to injury.

79

"Just leave me alone," I grumbled, but Ethan pulled his old trick again, stopping me, kissing me. The way he did at the bar the other night. He wanted so badly for our former connection to ignite and us to click again, and I put up a wall. But this time, I was weak. This time, it came on the heels of bad news from the pediatrician. This time, I melted into him the way I always used to.

Ethan deepened the kiss, and it took my breath away. I needed his comfort so badly and he didn't even know it. I let him own me for the moment, resting my hands on his shoulders and kissing him back. It felt like no time had passed, like we were always meant to be here doing this. I wanted this, needed this. So I gave in and tangled my fingers in his hair and tried to forget we were at work and that this was against hospital policy, or that we had a child together whom I had kept secret.

I whimpered, and he read me like a book, scooping me up behind the thighs and setting me on the edge of the empty patient bed. The mattress was too firm, but we wouldn't be sleeping.

He started to peel my scrubs off, kissing my collar bone, and I felt a thrill race down my spine. With practiced ease, he removed my bra and the fabric puddled on the floor. "We should stop," I panted, not meaning it.

"No, we shouldn't," he growled against my skin as he teased my nipples with his teeth and I whimpered again, arching into him. "I want you so bad." Ethan's hands worked miracles on my curves, eliciting moans and whimpers of pleasure. He massaged my clit, and I opened myself to receive it.

"Ethan," I moaned as he teased my core, coaxing out my wetness before he plunged his fingers deep inside me. I leaned back on my elbows, gripping the sheets with white-knuckled hands. Heat pooled between my legs, and I couldn't stop the moans that escaped my lips.

"You're so wet," he purred, and I blushed deep but didn't deny it. "I've missed you."

"I missed you too," I panted as he stroked me, curling his fingers just so. I arched my back, trying to get closer, needing more. While he worked my pussy with one hand, he undid the tie on his scrubs with the other then pulled his hard length out and stroked it.

"Like we used to?" he asked, and I nodded, biting my lip.

He didn't make me wait long. Ethan pushed my thighs wider and thrust into me in one smooth move, filling me to the hilt. We both moaned at the contact, our bodies rejoining as if they had been apart for far too long. He began to move, and I matched his pace as if we had never been apart all these years. I bit my lip, wanting to stay quiet, but I was never good at that during sex and the pleasure was too much.

When my moans and whimpers got too loud, he covered my mouth with his and I let him swallow the groans and the way I called his name. His thrusts were deep and primal, claiming me like he always did. I wrapped my legs around his waist and he pushed deeper, provoking a loud whimper from me. "Shh," he murmured against my ear, picking up the pace. I clamped my thighs tighter around his waist as the pressure built between my legs.

"I'm almost there," I panted, clutching at the sheets as the orgasm barreled toward me like a freight train.

"Me too," he said, his voice strained. His movements became more urgent, driving me over the edge as I whimpered and my body spasmed around him. He slowed, letting me enjoy the convulsions before pulling out and gripping his cock hard. His dick spat the seed out, and he leaned forward, making sure it dripped to the floor, not all over his scrubs or mine. I collapsed onto the bed, heaving.

I knew this was only leading him on. He was confessing his love to me, telling me how he wanted to make this work and try again. I was lying to him and keeping a secret that would destroy his heart and ruin any chance I had. I hated it, but I loved him still, and more than ever, I needed him by my side. I didn't want to ruin the budding relationship, not so soon. Not when it felt so good to be loved again.

He offered me a hand and I sat up. "We should leave separately. Don't want to get caught..." He leaned down and kissed me roughly. "Dinner at my place tomorrow?"

I nodded numbly, but I didn't know if I'd go through with it. I felt too guilty. He smiled and tucked his dick away, then handed me my clothes and used a paper towel to wipe up the floor. The room would have to be sterilized again before a patient came in here, which meant one of us would have to have a good reason for why we were asking the orderlies to clean what should have been a clean room.

It was what was on my mind when he kissed my cheek and said goodbye, then vanished. At this point, I was my own worst enemy and I couldn't even fight myself. Ethan Matthews was off limits to my heart, or he should have been. Having hidden this secret meant my love was nothing but a Trojan horse to his love. I'd infiltrate and destroy, and it wouldn't even matter that my desire for him and affection were genuine. I had ruined any chance for a future with him with the choices and mistakes I'd made in the past.

None of this should have been happening, and if I didn't put a stop to it, it was going to snowball out of control and like a ticking time bomb, it would explode in my face and hurt us both. I had to stop that from happening, but first, I had to have control of myself and my desire for him.

14

ETHAN

I stood at the nurses' station with my chart and watched the room I just left. Lily didn't pull away from me this time the way I feared she might, and I never expected that kiss to go that far. But I wasn't disappointed that it had. Her irrational behavior was another story. I was confused by the way she was acting. The swing between hot and cold made my head spin. And it made me feel guilty.

I had apologized to her and I meant it, but maybe the way I hurt her years ago really had messed with her. The back and forth in her demeanor showed she was wrestling internally with something, and I was willing to bet it had to do with me. One minute, she was pleasant and willing to go to dinner with me and the next, she was angry and holding a grudge over something I had already apologized for.

When the door swung open and she walked out looking fresh and put together, I relaxed a little. I had already divulged my desire to date Lily to the HR rep, but that didn't excuse the sex we just had. Even if we were approved and on file as being a couple, I was positive hospital administration would frown on sex on hospital property, especially while we were on the clock. But it didn't appear that anyone noticed how I left the room and moments later, Lily did.

She approached me at the counter and her stiff posture warned me off. The woman who was putty in my hands moments ago had vanished and Dr. Lily Carter had returned.

"So, dinner at my place tomorrow?" I asked, not even caring that one of the nurses nearby might hear. This was different from last time at St. Anne's when we had to sneak around. Back then, all I cared about was my career. Having spent so long alone, however, I knew the value of having a woman I loved in my life. Which was why I was doing things the right way this time.

"I'm not sure, Dr. Matthews. I'll have to see..." Her shoulders stayed squared, but her face drooped.

"Girl, a man that hot asks you out, you go." One of the nurses snickered and winked at me as she walked past and out into the hallway.

Lily didn't seem to appreciate the unsolicited comment, but I thought it was comical. I smiled and took a step back to offer her some space. "I'll let you think it over. Just text me if you are interested." I pulled out my business card from my lab coat pocket and laid it on the counter in front of her. She picked it up and studied it but said nothing. "I'll see you later."

"Yeah, later..." she mumbled, and I walked away.

It was like trying to decipher hieroglyphics on the wall of a cave. Lily was an enigma I needed to understand, and I wouldn't quit until I did. Even if it meant swallowing my pride and pushing my sleeves up to do hard emotional work with her and fix what I broke.

I headed down toward surgical to check in on a patient I had diagnosed with gallstones and my phone rang. I reached into my pocket and pulled it out and immediately recognized the phone number. It was the retirement community where my father lived and that probably wasn't a good thing, so I answered it.

"Dr. Matthews speaking."

"Hi, Ethan, this is Stella from Sunshine Village. I'm calling about your father." Stella was a middle-aged woman with bright red hair and freckles on her face. They made her look ten years younger.

"Oh, hey, Stella. What's up?" I nodded at a passing nurse who waved at me and turned toward my patient's room.

"Well, Thomas took a fall this morning in the shower. The nurse's aide who was with him said he was being stubborn again, demanding to do things on his own and refusing help. We are going to take him to St. Anne's for some X-rays, but we might be looking at a broken hip." Stella's news was a blow to my good mood and sucked the last vestiges of afterglow right out of my body.

"Wow, is he in pain?" I asked, realizing I wasn't going to be checking on my patient after all. My mind flew into action, making a list of things I'd have to have rescheduled and tasked to other doctors this afternoon. It sounded like I'd be sitting in an emergency room with Mom the rest of the day.

"He is, but we've given him some narcotics. He's a bit belligerent right now, but we're hoping the pain meds calm that down too." She chuckled, and I rolled my eyes. I knew just what a pain in the butt my dad could be at times.

"How long until the transport is ready?" I wished they would bring him to Mountain View, but hiring an ambulance to bring him all the way across Denver to the more elite hospital was out of the question for the small retirement community. The best I could do was to have him transferred once he was admitted, and then it would be on my dime, not theirs.

"They'll be here in thirty minutes, so you have a bit of time to get Barbra and meet him there." She sighed. "I'm sorry this happened. If only he would just let us help him. Maybe you can talk to him about not being so feisty and demanding independence. There's a reason he moved in here. He needs help with things."

I backtracked on my walk toward the patient and diverted to my office where I sat behind my desk. "I don't blame you one bit. He is definitely a little prideful and stubborn. I'm sure if he'd have let the nurse help him in the shower, he wouldn't have fallen. I'll get Mom and meet the ambulance over there. Thanks for letting me know, Stella."

"No problem, Dr. Matthews. Have a good day. We'll update you if there is any change."

We hung up, and I sent out a slew of text messages to my nursing staff, interns, and a colleague who would take over my rounds for the day. A broken him wouldn't just be a quick in and out for him. Hip surgery in a man my father's age sometimes took six months to come back from, longer if the patient wasn't well off before needing the surgery. And sometimes, men his age never came back. Sometimes, they died.

I pushed those thoughts from my head and gathered a few things from my desk before heading out. Any thought of Lily and the incredible sex we just had was pushed from my head as I drove home. Mom was ready, having already received a call from Stella. She sat on the porch swing with her sweater draped over her arm in case it was cold in the emergency room. When I pulled up, she stood and shuffled toward the car.

Before I could even climb out to walk with her, she was at the passenger door. I hit the unlock button, and she opened the door and climbed in. She looked worried. Even she knew how scary something like this could be for a man his age.

"It's going to be okay, Mom. We'll get the best doctors we can on his case. I can even have him transferred to Mountain View and my team can handle things if you want." I reached for her hand, and she shut the door before clasping my hand in hers.

"He'll be angry about that. You know he doesn't like to be babied." Her lip trembled as she spoke, and I felt her pain. Her partner of more than fifty years was aging and struggling, and eventually, they'd have to say goodbye.

"Buckle up. I need to drive." I patted her knee and took my hand back.

Thirty minutes later, we were walking into the emergency department at St. Anne's. It was a blast from the past. Familiar faces surrounded us as we signed in and were escorted to Dad's exam room. The staff all had encouraging things to say, but I found myself strangely craving Lily's presence, as if having her here would calm me more, anchor me in the hope that everything would be okay.

Mom sat by Dad's bedside and held his hand, but he was sedated, snoring loudly. I hovered by the door waiting for the doctor to come in, and I almost pounced on him when he did. He was young, probably a fourth-year resident with little experience, but thankfully, he was only here to triage and diagnose. The surgeon would be doing the real work.

"So, you knocked him out?" I asked, and he chuckled.

"Yes, he was a handful and he was in pain, so it was a no-brainer." The man thrust his hand out at me. "Dr. Garber."

I shook his hand. "Dr. Matthews... Thomas is my father. This is my mother, Barbra." I nodded at Mom, who didn't even look up or try to smile. She had tears in her eyes and was trying to put on a brave front.

"Well, this is a cut and dry diagnosis. He has two breaks in his hip area—a femoral neck fracture and one on the ilium. The ilium will heal on its own as long as he's careful, but the hip is going to need rods or he'll never walk again." The pronouncement was about as bad as it got.

I turned to look at my dad and wondered if he would come out of this or not. "Thanks, Doc. I think we'd like a minute alone to discuss this."

"Of course, take the time you need. I'll be available if you have questions. We'll get him admitted as soon as possible." The doctor left the room, and I stood next to Dad's bed on the opposite side as Mom. She sniffled and looked up at me and smiled.

"When you love someone, you care for them even in their sickness..." Her thoughtful comment made me think of Lily and whatever was going on with her. Mom hadn't caused Dad's hip to break, but she was here to help him. I had caused Lily's heart to break, and it made me feel awful. I had to be there to help her even when she lashed out at me in anger. It was the right thing.

"You're right, Mom, and we both love him and we'll take care of him." I sat on the edge of the bed and braced myself for her to fall apart. I knew it was coming. I just didn't know when. Until then, all I could do was be a strong, steady presence to reassure her and help her. And it was good practice for when I had to sit next to Lily and take her tongue lashings. She deserved a calm man to love her, and I resolved to let this situation teach me how to be that for her.

Otherwise, I didn't deserve her.

15

LILY

Noah curled into my side and coughed again, a coughing fit that worried me. I'd already been on the phone to his pediatrician twice this morning for suggestions as to what to do, but Dr. Butler's advice was to have Noah rest. It had only been a few days since he ordered the medications, and while Noah's blood pressure issue was under control, his wheezing was getting worse.

"Mommy, I not feel good." His little face was pale, but Dr. Butler insisted we needed a bit more time for the medication to work. He was already researching surgeons and looking for the best specialist for Noah. With my health care plan, the hospital would practically pay for everything anyway. All I cared about was having my son happy and healthy, which right now, he was definitely neither of those two things.

"I know, baby. Mommy called the doctor, okay? We're going to help you feel better really soon." The timeline for his surgery had been moved up from two weeks to as soon as possible. If Noah's wheezing got worse, we could end up with an emergency situation. I was tempted just to take him to the emergency room at St Anne's anyway to get a second opinion.

"When can I feel better? I want to jump on Nana's champoline." The comical way he mixed up the words made me smile.

"It's called a trampoline, buddy, and really, really soon, okay?" I brushed the hair out of his eyes and noticed he was moist with sweat, a symptom of how hard his body was working. My gut told me to take him in, but I wanted to trust Dr. Butler's expertise.

My phone buzzed, and I unlocked it again. Ethan had been texting me casually while he worked. He knew I was off today for personal reasons, and he seemed concerned about me, though I had told him a number of times that I wasn't sick.

Ethan 10:48 AM: I could bring you some soup at lunch time if you want.

It was sweet of him to offer, but we had already eaten an early lunch because Noah was hungry. He hadn't even eaten breakfast because of his tummy hurting, so I made him a grilled cheese and we'd only just finished and cleaned up. I'd been reading him picture books for a few minutes.

Lily 10:48 AM: I'm fine, really. I told you I just took a personal day to deal with something. Thank you, though.

I went back to reading to Noah, who looked annoyed at me for taking a break from the book to respond to Ethan. With my phone in my lap, Noah curled up next to me holding the book I read to him about shapes and colors. I saw two more messages from Ethan but ignored them because I noticed Noah getting tired. Sleeping was the best thing for him right now because if he was sleeping, he wasn't aware of his own suffering, nor was he jumping around or worsening the condition.

"You getting sleepy, buddy?" I asked, and he shook his head defiantly.

"I not tired. You read the book to me." He crossed his arms over his chest and pouted, and I set the book aside.

"I know you think you're not tired, but I see sleepy eyes." I scooped him up and grabbed my phone, and we headed upstairs to the bedroom. I'd been letting him sleep in my bed with me ever since we moved back in with Mom and Dad because I'd been worried about him. I didn't know how I'd fare when I finally got my own place and he wanted to sleep in his own bed.

"Nana said ice cream for supper." He scrunched his nose and patted my cheek, and I took his glasses off him and set him on the side of the bed.

"Nana is silly. You need to eat healthy food first." I winked at him. "Need to potty first?" I asked, and he scowled.

"No." Grumpy and frustrated with me, he crawled up onto the pillow and lay down. I took his baby blanket and covered him in it. He'd been attached to it ever since his surgery when it became his security blanket. When the one he used at the time got a hole, I went out and found an identical one and bought five more, just in case something happened to it again. I figured I couldn't be too careful, and by the time he outgrew the need for it, they'd all be used up.

"Want me to cuddle?" I asked, and he turned his back to me, so I lay down in bed next to him quietly while I waited for sleep to claim him. My phone buzzed a few more times. I figured it was all Ethan, waiting for me to respond, but I didn't know if I wanted to respond.

I'd done a lot of thinking about it, mostly at night when I should have been sleeping but I was wide awake with insomnia thanks to the anxiety I'd been having. Ethan was Noah's father, and he had every right to know what was going on. It was selfish of me on the part of both Noah and Ethan to continue skirting the issue and blaming it on the past every time I got flighty and scared he was close to figuring it out.

Yes, we had reconnected, and my God, was it amazing. I wanted to keep it, to savor the way he made me feel so wanted by chasing me and being so perfect—more perfect than ever. But it was only prolonging the torture for me and delaying the fact that my confession would end it. I was letting my own heart get carried away in desiring something that would never happen, and I had to stop. I opened my phone and read Ethan's messages.

Ethan 10:53 AM: I could stop by that bakery you love on Tower Road. Get you some of those scones you like so much.

Ethan 10:55 AM: Or I could bring you coffee? You like the espresso from Margret's still, right?"

Ethan 11:12 AM: I don't want to sound pushy. I was just hoping for some time with you. Were you still thinking of coming to dinner tonight?

Ethan 11:13 AM: It's okay if not. I just thought we were doing well with rekindling...

That last one got me. He felt it too, the warm intimacy when we were good together, and it wasn't just the sex. We'd had so few interactions outside of work, but when we had, he was showing himself to be the most amazing man on the planet. I, however, was showing myself to be so messed up, up and down, back and forth. Ethan deserved better, and I needed to show him better if I had any chance of convincing him I felt horrible and wanted to undo my past decisions. God knows, he'd shown me already.

Lily 11:24 AM: What are you doing for lunch? I can meet you.

I typed and sent the message and knew he'd reply instantly. I had to get this all off my chest. I originally thought telling him while going through this was going to make it worse for me, but the longer the symptoms Noah was having dragged on, the more I realized not telling Ethan was making it worse, not the other way around. I had to get it off my chest so I didn't worry about it and I could focus on my little boy—our little boy.

Whatever happened, happened. I couldn't change it. I made my choices, and they had consequences, and I knew I had to deal with those consequences now.

Ethan 11:25 AM: I'm going home to put food in the crock pot for dinner and grab a sandwich. Want to meet me there?

My heart skipped a beat. Telling him in public would have been hard enough. Telling him at home where he had the privacy to really blow up and get angry with me scared me. I was nervous, not responding immediately, and my thumbs hovered over the screen, shaking. But if I backed out now, I knew I'd never get the courage up to do it again. I glanced at Noah, whose eyes were shut, and knew it was the best thing for him. Tiny snores came from his slightly parted lips, and part of me broke. He deserved a chance to know his father.

Lily 11:27 AM: I'll be there in twenty.

I slipped from bed and grabbed my keys as I shoved my feet into my sandals. With my phone in my pocket, I jogged down the steps and into the kitchen where Mom sat. She looked up when I walked in.

"Hey, Noah's napping. Do you mind watching him while I run out for an errand? Call me as soon as he wakes up?" With his wheezing getting worse and his complaining of belly pain, I wanted someone watching him round the clock now.

"Of course. Go on," she said, gesturing with her hand. She didn't question what my "errand" was, and I didn't tell her. If I spoke about it, I'd change my mind.

Twenty minutes later, as promised, I was parked in Ethan's driveway, staring up at his house. His car was here too, maybe only for a few minutes before I pulled up. He might be getting lunch or he could be watching out the window, wondering why I was hesitating. My stomach churned, and I felt like I'd throw up, but I forced myself out of the car. My feet carried me to the door, and I shook a little as I rang the bell.

When he opened, he had a smile on his face and he reached for me. I let him pull me in for a hug, and I savored the closeness for those few seconds. I knew once I said what I'd come to say, I wouldn't be so lucky as to enjoy his embrace anymore.

"Ethan, there is something I need to talk to you about." Words were already forming in my thoughts, how I would say it, what I would say. My apology would mean little or nothing, and I doubted that even the fiercest love would be forgiving enough to listen without being angry or hurt. No doubt Ethan cared for me, but after this, we'd be civil with each other and any lasting intimacy we had would be shattered. He'd never trust me again.

"Alright, but I have something to say first." He shut the door and led me by the hand into the kitchen.

There was a smattering of canned goods open but empty on the counter next to the crockpot. A spoon with some sort of sauce on it lay next to them, and on the other side of the island was a stack of papers. Ethan walked right over to the stack of papers and picked them up with a huge grin.

"I know this is really insane and that things are awkward and still not the best between us, but I talked to HR." He turned and walked toward me as my eyebrows rose. "What happened last time can't happen again. We snuck around and we were stupid, and I didn't take care of things properly. This time, before we even start out, I wanted things done correctly so neither of us had regrets or risked our jobs.

"Mom gave me some good advice, and I intend to take it. Lily, real love goes beyond mistakes and failures. Both of us are human and both of us made mistakes before. I want you to know I will love you beyond all of that."

He handed me the papers, and I saw the title on the top of the first one. It read, *Declaration of Relationship for Excusal from Non-Fraternization Policy.* My eyes welled up with tears as I looked over the paper which he had already filled in and signed. I glanced through them as the tears started to fall, but I didn't know what to say. This man was offering me everything I wanted, and I was about to break his heart.

"Say something," he urged, but all I could do was cry. This time, I wasn't running away. I had to tell him he had a son.

Heaven help me...

16

ETHAN

The way Lily just stood there crying, holding the HR documents in her hands, made me wonder what she was thinking. Was she sad that I'd gone behind her back or over- whelmed with joy that I was doing the right thing? She was speech- less, and I was nervous she was going to rush away again. I stepped forward and took the papers from her hands and set them down on the counter, then cupped both of her cheeks and used my thumbs to brush away her tears.

"I told you I want to do this thing the right way this time, Lily. I know last time ended horribly because of my fears and insecurities. I want you to know I refuse to let my ego or pride get in the way this time. I went straight to HR the minute I saw you. I am in love with you and I want you in my life."

My words only made her cry harder, which further confused me. I leaned down and kissed her softly, and she reached up and wrapped her hands around my wrists. It wasn't a hesitant touch either. It was needy and desperate, as if she wanted to curl up inside my chest and hide from whatever emotion she was feeling, and I wanted her there. I wanted the space I had carved out for her to be filled by her presence and for her to feel safe.

"I do love you," I whispered, but she greedily kissed me again, then tangled her fingers in the hair at the back of my head. The more she kissed me, the harder I got, hungry to cement this moment of affection by being inside her. She was addictive and I was the addict, seeking the fix from whatever she was willing to give me.

I didn't even check the time. I walked her backward across the kitchen, kissing her the entire way, until we were passing through the living room. I wasn't watching where we were going, and we bumped into the couch. Lily whimpered and started unbuttoning my shirt, and I followed her lead. I tugged on her shirt and untucked it from her slacks. She raised her arms so I could pull it over her head. Her tits spilled from her bra when I unhooked it, and I grabbed one, kneading it.

"This time, we'll do it right. No sneaking around in secret," I told her, and she whined again. Her sniffling and soft cries felt so vulnerable to me, like this was healing a place in her heart that had been raw and wounded. And she was pliable, letting me mold her with my hands, yielding to my touch.

I undid her pants and shoved them down before shrugging out of my shirt, which I laid carefully over the back of the couch. As I lowered to my knees next to her, she panted, "Ethan, I..." But she didn't finish her sentence because I buried my face between her thighs and found her swelling nub. She tasted salty, and a little musky from her arousal. I didn't care. It was better than the finest wine ever could be.

"Shh, don't say a word," I murmured against her pussy, licking her clit, sucking on it like a ripe berry. "Just feel."

My tongue moved in circles, flicking and lapping at her wetness as she twisted and moaned above me. I kept up the pace until she started trembling, and she gripped my hair so tightly I thought she might rip it out by the roots.

"God, Ethan! There!" She panted, grinding her hips against my face, seeking more contact. I gave it to her gladly, tracing lazy S-shapes on her entrance with my tongue. Her juices were delicious, and when she lifted a leg over my shoulder, I was able to enjoy them more.

Lily arched her back and hissed in pleasure. "Oh, God, Ethan," she moaned, and I grinned. I lapped at her vulva, tickling her entrance with my tongue before zeroing in on her clit again. Lily gripped the cushions of the couch and moaned louder as I sucked and nipped her skin. I loved the way she writhed beneath my touch.

I didn't want to rush this. I wanted to draw it out as long as possible, to remind her why she was with me to begin with, of what she'd been missing for so long. I suckled her clit into my mouth, flicking it rapidly with my tongue while slipping two fingers inside her soaking wet pussy. Her cries of pleasure were music to my ears as she rocked back and forth on my fingers, matching my rhythm. Lily was so wet that my fingers effortlessly slid in and out of her, coating them in her arousal. I curled my fingers, searching for her sweet spot, and when I found it, she arched her back and grunted something unintelligible as her orgasm crashed over her.

Wave after convulsive wave racked her body until her knee gave out and her weight rested on my shoulder. I bore up under her frame and held her there, pinned against the couch as I continued to thrust my fingers into her. She whimpered and returned her hands to my head where her fingers clawed away at my scalp. Her pussy contracted and tightened again and again on my fingers until the spasms stopped and her weight lifted.

She was breathless, panting and pulling me upward by the jaw. I rose and let her leg slide from my shoulder, and on the way up, I dropped my pants. They fell to the floor with a thud, but not before I retrieved the condom from my back pocket. After dumping my load onto her stomach and the floor the last two times, I made the conscious decision to have a condom on me at all times because I wanted to enjoy it, not waste the sensation.

"Ethan, I…" she said again, and I got the feeling she was going to bolt or say something I didn't want to hear.

"Shh," I told her as I tore open the condom wrapper and rolled it on.

Her eyes were drawn to thin slits, emotion still filling them. But it didn't look like love and adoration. It looked like grief or mourning. Like she was heartbroken. I held her gaze as I lifted one of her legs and positioned myself at her entrance.

"I'm not going anywhere ever again. You can let your heart trust that now, Lily." I pushed in slowly, eyes locked on hers, and she moaned softly. Her body wrapped around mine like a glove. It felt so damn good to be here again, inside her.

"Ethan, I…" she tried again. I silenced her with a kiss as I thrust all the way in, bottoming out inside her wet heat. She tasted like regret and tears, but also something else. Hope.

As I began to move, she wrapped her arms around my neck and kissed me back, tears streaming down her face. I held her close, stroking in and out of her, just as slow as I could stand it, until our movements fell into rhythm.

"I love you," I whispered against her ear. "I always have." Lily tensed in my arms but didn't pull away. Instead, she angled her hips up, trying to meet my thrusts. She had missed me as much as I'd missed her. That was evident with every moan and gasp that escaped her lips.

"Ethan…" She panted, tightening around me, and her breathing grew thready.

"What is it?" I asked her, kissing her neck and jawline. Being inside her had never felt so good. Every agonizingly slow thrust was more exquisite than the previous, and I knew I wouldn't last much longer.

"I… I love you too. Never stopped loving you," she sobbed against me, and my heart swelled with happiness. Today was a good fucking day.

"About damn time you admitted it," I said with a grin, picking up speed. Five years of pent-up frustration and lust surged through me as I pounded into her, harder and harder, all while consumed by the knowledge that she was mine again. Lily's legs wrapped around my waist, holding me close as she tried to get me deeper inside her.

"Oh, God, Ethan, I'm going to…" She moaned, and I felt her pussy clench around me again. "Yes!" she cried out and threw her head back, eyes squeezed shut as her orgasm hit. I didn't slow my relentless assault on her body even when she bit my shoulder and cried out.

She was mine, and I was hers, and nothing was going to come between us again. I would make sure of that. I felt her continue to ride out her orgasm, and when she finally calmed down, I kissed her as my body shuddered. Climax tore through me, making me jolt and shudder. I grunted and held her against myself tightly, and she panted and tried to catch her breath.

I stayed there buried inside her for a few seconds, breathing in the scent of her perfume or shampoo. It was flowery and sweet, and so intoxicating I didn't want to pull away. It was obvious to me that she had a favorable opinion of my decision to inform HR preemptively. She didn't have to say it. Her response to my touch was enough.

When I pulled away and out of her, she whimpered and clung to me, so I stayed close. I kissed her forehead and then her lips, and she sighed softly. The tears were gone, but when I looked into her eyes, the emotion was not.

"Ethan, we have to talk." When Lily bit her lower lip, I knew something was wrong. But for the first time since she had returned to my life, she wasn't running away. She was staying to talk it out. I found myself a little uneasy about it as I tugged the condom off and tied it shut.

"I know I made that decision to talk to HR without you, but I just wanted to make sure I was doing things right this time." I figured if I talked first, whatever it was wouldn't seem so pressing to her. That she'd relax and calm down a little. Judging by the way she scurried to grab her clothes and dress while I stuffed the full condom back into the foil wrapper, she was feeling antsy.

"No, it's not that," she mumbled, balancing on one foot, then the other as she put on her panties and slacks.

"And I know we haven't even discussed whether we are really in a relationship or if this is casual sex yet, but you know I love you. You know I want you to marry you someday. That never changed..." I tossed the condom and returned to put my own pants back on, but she was fussing with the hook on her bra, so I paused to help her hook it shut, then let my hands slide around to the front to grope her perfect, fleshy globes as I kissed her cheek.

"No, Ethan, there's something I need to say." She pushed my hands away gently, and I felt like she was going to say this was a mistake, that it needed to stop. Her heart was so fragile, and I had broken it, and what if I was moving too fast?

"I know what you're thinking, but I promise this time will be different, and I'm willing to do anything it takes to—"

"No, Ethan. Please." She huffed and tugged her shirt on, then jammed her feet into her shoes, discarded when I shucked her pants. "I need to tell you something. There's something you don't know. When I left Denver I was—" Her phone started to ring, and she tensed. She shook her head and reached into her pocket and pulled it out, and her face went pale.

"Are you okay?" I asked, but as I buckled my belt, she turned and answered the call with her back toward me. I picked up my shirt and continued dressing as she did.

"Mom...? Yeah, I'm.... He what!" She sounded startled and a bit frantic. "And he's not breathing right? Oh, my God... I'm coming. I'll be there in five minutes. Call 9-1-1." Lily punched her phone and patted her pocket and bolted toward the door.

"Is everything okay? Do you need me?"

"I can't!" she spat. "I have to go." And then she was gone, rushing out the door and vanishing. I hurried to the door and watched her car back out of my driveway hastily. She laid rubber and her tires squealed on the pavement as she peeled out. Whatever was happening sounded serious, and dangerous. I tried calling, but she ignored it, probably wisely. As upset as she seemed, taking a call while driving wasn't safe.

But now I was worried—about what was happening right now, but also about what she felt she had to tell me. It didn't sound good, and I didn't like that.

I hoped everything was okay.

17

LILY

I rushed out of Ethan's house and to my car. Gone was any idea of telling him he was a father because the only thing I could think about was my little boy. Mom's call had me so panicked, I was speeding and praying I didn't get caught by a cop. I should have called an ambulance but there were complications. Not only would they have taken him straight to Mountain View, but I also wouldn't have been there to help them fully understand his condition. They would have called Ethan in for a diagnostic consultation.

But I also wanted to be with him every step of the way. With his fears, he needed me. Mom sounded concerned and not panicked, so I trusted my gut and drove like the wind. My little boy was more important to me than anything in the world, and everything else could wait.

Whipping into the driveway, I had the car off and the door open before I was even fully stopped. I raced to the front door and fumbled with my key in the dark, and before I got it unlocked, Dad was there opening for me.

"Where is he?" I asked, rushing past him, but he didn't need to answer. Mom had Noah on the couch lying down with a book in hand. I hurried to his side and dropped to my knees next to him. I immediately knew he wasn't oxygenating properly. "Hey, buddy," I cooed, finding his wrist with my index and middle finger so I could check his pulse.

"Mommy..." he croaked, but he didn't smile. "My belly hurts."

"What happened?" I demanded of my mother and then turned behind me and reached to the coffee table where Noah's portable blood pressure cuff lay.

Mom grimaced and sat a little straighter as I slid the cuff on his spindly arm and pressed the start button. She sighed and said, "He was napping, Lily. I just heard a crash, and I ran upstairs to see what was going on. Noah was jumping on the bed, and the lamp fell over and broke. I made him get down right away, but he's been wheezing even more and saying his belly really hurts."

The cuff hissed and pumped, and I held it in place until it inflated on his bicep. "Noah, baby, why were you jumping on the bed?" I frowned, but not at him. He was just a little boy being told not to be a little boy. He didn't know any better. I frowned because of the situation and how bad his wheezing sounded now.

Noah only coughed in response and laid his book down. He stared up at me with giant eyes and blinked slowly like he was sleepy. His lips weren't bright pink like they should have been, more tinged with blue from lower oxygen saturation. The blood pressure readout was way too high, which meant the meds weren't controlling it right now, and that was bad news. It meant his jumping up and down had only caused the hernia to get worse.

"Wow, okay," I sighed. "I have to take him to the hospital." I stood abruptly and turned. "Watch him while I grab a bag."

Mom muttered a response I didn't pay attention to, and I ran up the stairs two at a time to the bedroom. Dad followed along behind me, but I had a few changes of clothing for myself and several of Noah's favorite toys and books in the bag before he opened the door.

"Where will we take him?" he asked as if he were planning to go along. The gesture was loving, but I was too scared to do much more than take it for granted and shake my head. Moments like this made

SILVER FOX'S SECRET BABY

me lose my mind with worry. I'd be the first to admit I didn't make good choices all the time.

"I have to go to St. Anne's. This time of day, Dr. Butler will be seeing patients and won't be on the clock for a consult." I rushed around the room grabbing my toiletries and more things for Noah as I spoke. "The doctors at Mountain View don't know me well enough to trust my judgment as a doctor. They'll think I'm a panicking parent. But at St. Anne's, they know me."

Dad stood stoically in the doorway leaning on the jamb, and I yanked the zipper shut and hefted the bag to my shoulder. "Are you sure St. Anne's is the right place? Mountain View has a larger pediatrics department." His soft protest angered me.

I couldn't take Noah there. I wouldn't. They would call Ethan for a consult and everything would explode. I had to be able to tell Ethan about Noah in my own way, not in an emergency room with a hundred people around us.

"St. Anne's is a great hospital, Dad. I worked there, remember? I know the staff. They have the capability to do this." When I got to the door, he backed up so I could walk past, and I went straight to the bathroom to grab our toothbrushes. "Besides, it's my choice as his parent."

I saw the wind leave Dad's sails as I made my independence obvious to him, and concern deepened in his eyes.

"Lillian, are you sure you're not just avoiding Mountain View because you don't want Dr. Matthews to see his own son? You haven't told him anything and now you'll go to a less qualified hospital to keep the two apart?"

The hammer hit the nail on the head and I inwardly winced. Dad was one hundred percent right, but he didn't understand why this was the only choice. Ethan would be crushed. I couldn't do that to him. Not to mention a parent isn't legally allowed to treat their child. It would put him in an impossible situation because I knew this was something that needed to be dealt with quickly, and to replace Ethan with a different doctor would mean a delay that would be horrible for Noah.

"I made my decision, Dad." I should have just taken Noah to the emergency room when the wheezing first started, when it wasn't urgent and pressing. St. Anne's would have called in their specialists and this would have been done in a relaxed manner. I was beginning to doubt my original trust in Dr. Butler.

I jogged down the steps and over to where Mom had Noah sitting up. She was lacing his shoes on and he was shivering.

"Are you cold, buddy?" I pressed my hand to his forehead and he was cool, but he was moist with sweat. His body was chilled from the exertion of just sitting up and having to breathe. He probably also had some anxiety when he heard me tell Mom he needed to go to the hospital.

"I don't wanna go," Noah whined, and Mom put her arm around him.

"Nana will go with you, okay, baby?" She kissed his forehead, and he grimaced and tried to pull away, but it caused a coughing fit.

Sitting beside him, I dropped the bag on the floor at our feet and slid him onto my lap. I cradled him and talked him through the coughing until he was breathing a bit easier, and Mom and Dad hovered the entire time.

"Maybe we should just call an ambulance." Mom's hand was reaching for her phone on the coffee table next to Noah's cuff before I even answered.

"No, Mom," I said firmly. "I will drive him. An ambulance will take another thirty minutes to get here and then thirty to the hospital. If we get in my car now, we can be there in twenty." The logic seemed to make sense to her, which made me breathe a sigh of relief. Any ambulance on this side of Denver would take him where I didn't want him to go.

Dad pulled his keys out of his pocket and jingled them. "Let me drive then, Lily. You can sit in back by Noah and help him better than either Mom or I could." I was still afraid he would do the wrong thing and take Noah to Mountain View. Sometimes, Dad did what he wanted to do when I didn't agree with it at all. Like the time he gave Noah too much caffeine late at night and I had no sleep before work.

"St. Anne's," I said defensively. Dad was a parent, and parents usually do what they want, but I trusted that he would respect me.

"If that's where you want to go. Anywhere is better than here." He offered me his hand, and I stood with Noah in one arm and used Dad's hand as support.

We hurried to the car, and Mom took a few minutes to shut off the lights and lock up. By the time I had Noah in his booster seat, we were all loaded and Dad was pulling out. He took a second to shut my car door before he climbed in, otherwise there would have been a minor collision.

I kept an eye on Noah's face the entire drive. The darker blue his lips were, the worse it was getting, but I didn't know if I was overreacting. I talked to him softly but he was limp and lethargic, both signs his breathing wasn't right and his blood pressure was too high. In my haste, I'd left his cuff on the table and without my cuff and stethoscope, I couldn't take it manually.

"Go faster, Dad," I whimpered, and I clung to the booster seat to avoid crying. Noah needed me to be strong now. If he saw me freaking out, it would make him more upset which would affect both his already-taxed breathing and his too-high blood pressure. Hopefully, they would get him in for his surgery tonight and this would be a matter of helping my little boy deal with his fear while recovering.

18

ETHAN

L ily breezed out of my room so fast it left me wondering what the hell happened. From what I gathered from the one-sided phone conversation I'd overheard, someone she cared about had done something and was having trouble breathing. I sat on the foot of the bed wondering just who that "someone" might be. A few times over the past several weeks, I had feared she was dating someone else. But Lily was too classy for that. She would never be a cheater.

Which left only one possible assumption. Lily had no brothers, only Kate, her younger sister. Which meant the person struggling with a health issue was most likely her father. I couldn't see Kate getting married, but if she did, I didn't see Lily being the type of doting sister-in-law who would rush off after incredible sex like that without any explanation. Her dad must have been suffering for a while and things took a turn for the worse.

That made me think of my ailing father and Mom, who lay in bed two doors down. She was running a mild fever earlier this afternoon. I had given her some Tylenol to lower the fever and help her body aches. I assumed it was a cold or the flu, and she just wanted to rest.

Lily having her own struggles with aging parents only made me feel more connected to her, more in sync.

I put the rest of my clothing back on and decided to check on Mom. It had been long enough that the medication would be wearing off, if it hadn't fully worn off already. She would want me to get her more if the fever hadn't abated. And she might be hungry or thirsty. Even on her good days, I did a lot of these things for her just because I cared. But when she was ill, I played nurse round the clock, and I didn't mind doing it.

Tapping on her door, I pushed it open. "Just me, Mom." I leaned in and saw her lying on her side looking at me. The light was on low, casting an eerie glow over her face. Long shadows stretched toward her chin, and she blinked slowly.

"I'm awake." She didn't sound like herself. She sounded melancholy, and I knew why. Dad had been in so much pain following his surgery, he hadn't been as communicative. His calls lasted only a few minutes when he even made them, and he could only take visitors for an hour or so before he had to lie back down in bed. She missed him.

"How are you feeling?" I asked, tiptoeing to the nightstand. Mom's glass of water was empty and her lips looked dry.

"I'm tired and my body hurts. I think this cold is kicking my butt." Her usual happy demeanor had been replaced with a sullen expression and sadness. Seeing how she was so depressed over not being able to be with Dad or help him made my heart hurt for her, and for Lily.

I pictured her rushing to the ER to help her father, only to be told to sit down and be the loved one, not pretend to be the doctor. How many times had I been told that myself when it came to my parents? It was one of the most difficult things for a doctor—to know what to do and how to do it, to alleviate your loved one's suffering but being unable to do a thing because of state laws.

"Well, let's get you better." I grabbed a second pillow from the closet and walked to Mom's side. "Being a bit more upright will help your sinuses to drain better and keep the mucus out of your throat. Might even help your coughing to be more effective."

She struggled to sit up while I fluffed her pillow and added the second one, and I made sure she was back in a comfortable position when I was done. "I'll get you some more water and another round of pills."

I started to back away, but she grabbed my wrist. "Stay," she muttered, and I noticed the tears in her eyes.

"Of course." I sat on the edge of the mattress and let her hold my hand. I hated seeing her like this. Not just the sickness, but the sadness. She and Dad had been married for more than five decades. They were each other's everything, and now they were separated and hurting.

"What will I do?" she asked timidly, but I didn't understand her question.

"What do you mean, Mom? About the cold? Or about..."

"About Tom." She blinked, and tears ran down her face. "What if he doesn't make it? What will I do, Ethan? I haven't been alone since nineteen sixty-nine. I don't even remember what it feels like to be alone."

Her words made my heartache worse. A man in my position had so many reasons to run from that question. If Dad didn't make it out of this thing with his hip, I'd have to watch my mother grieve her life partner. She'd be alone and hurting and no one would be here to truly console that pain because I couldn't replace him.

And I would lose my father too. He might not have always been the perfect father, but I looked up to him and respected him. I knew now as an adult son things I didn't know when I was a child, reasons he made choices for me I didn't like. He lived a hard life before I was old enough to understand what "hard" was. I respected his choices now.

And most of all, knowing my mom was going to end up dying after my father, that she'd be lonely and need me more than ever reminded me that I had no one. No love of my life, no wife, no children, no family. I had friends, but they weren't the sort of people who took care of you in your older years. Friends visit, but when they leave, who takes care of you?

"He's going to pull through. It's the only thing we can allow ourselves to think right now. If we give up hope before he's even had a chance to show us what a fighter he is, we won't be able to be there for him when he needs us."

She pushed herself up a little straighter and shook her head. "I know you're right, but the doctor said some patients never come back. Sometimes they die because the rehab afterward is so difficult. Ethan, I don't want to be alone."

I didn't want to be alone either. I wasn't naive enough to think my parents would live forever, but caring for them the past few years had taken the focus off myself and my loneliness. I wasn't as lonely because I had been busy caring for them. Now I realized that they wouldn't always be here and that I would be completely alone then. It made those precious moments with Lily seem even more sacred. She was who I wanted to actually grow old with.

"Those people often don't have family or support systems either." I stood and picked up her glass. "And we're here for him. We're going to be by his side as much as the nursing home staff will let us. In a few days, they will force him to get out of bed and start therapy. He'll need us there then. So will they." I chuckled because I knew how grumpy Dad was going to be in pain and being forced to try to stand up.

That brought a small smile to Mom's lips too because she knew him better than anyone. She had loved him for decades and had to tolerate his moody side for far longer than I had.

"I'm going to fill your water up, alright? I'll bring you more medicine and a snack." I headed to the door, but she cleared her throat.

"No snack. I'm not feeling hungry. Just the water is fine."

I nodded at her and walked out the door. The cloud hung over my head as I filled her glass and got her more medication. This whole situation was making my future look very bleak. I didn't want to grow old alone and have no one, and unless I did something about that, it was definitely in my future. It made me want to be reckless and impulsive, but safe.

I wanted to propose to Lily.

We had only just been attempting to work things out, but we had history. We were in love. What we shared years ago was there beneath the surface just waiting to explode into our present and surprise us both. I knew it. I loved her and I didn't want to be without her. I just didn't know how she'd take it. Especially if she was dealing with her own issues in her family.

With the glass full and pills in my hand, I went back to the bedroom where Mom was lightly dozing. She roused when I walked in and gave me the same slow-eyed blink as last time I came in. She looked frail and weak, not the robust, bold woman I remembered. Time had aged her and sapped her of vitality, and I was determined that before life did that to me, I would live it to the fullest.

"Here you go, Mom." I held out the pills, and she held her palm open for me to place them. She took them, but I had to help her steady the glass at her lips before sitting it on the nightstand.

"Thank you, dear." She patted my hand and yawned.

"Mom, can I ask your opinion about something?" I didn't sit this time, seeing that she wanted to rest now. I probably should have just let her rest, but with an idea this insane, if I was being too irrational, my mother would tell me.

"Yes, of course." Her hands folded together over her belly and she leaned her head back on the pillow.

"I want to marry Lily. She has been the one thing in my life that I ever thought was good. I messed it up a while back, but I'm getting this amazing second chance and I don't want to wait. I want to ask her to marry me. What do you think? Am I crazy?"

Mom's small smile helped me relax as she said, "Well, if you were twenty, I'd think you were crazy. If you were thirty and you didn't know her, I'd say you were crazy." She yawned again and covered her mouth then went on. "But you're forty years old, almost forty-one. You have history with this woman. You love her, that much is obvious. When a man loves a woman at your age, he doesn't take risks or wait around."

It wasn't exactly her blessing to go for it, but her message was clear. I wasn't getting any younger. As it was, even if I lived to be ninety, the most I could hope for was to see my children and grandchildren. I had spent too much of my life focusing on my career and making mistakes. I needed a partner now, and to care for me when I was older. Lily was the woman I wanted.

"Thanks, Mom." I leaned down and kissed her forehead and flipped her nightstand light off. Then I let myself out and turned toward my bedroom to get my shoes. Worries about Lily and what she was going through plagued me, and I called her to see if she needed anything, but her phone went straight to voicemail. So I put my shoes on and replaced my tie. I left my phone on full volume, though, just in case she called. And as I drove back to work, I thought about how and when I would propose.

I was going to shoot my shot, even if I missed the target. What could it hurt? If she said no, I could try again later, after we built something magical again. If she said yes, then she was mine forever.

19

LILY

Wmark hen we walked through the doors of the emergency
department at St. Anne's with Dad carrying Noah,
several staff members took notice immediately. I knew
they recognized me, judging by the looks on their faces. One of the
nurses, Amy, and I had been very close when I worked here. She was
the first to reach us.

"What's going on?" she asked as she took Noah's wrist and checked
his pulse.

"He was born with congenital diaphragmatic hernia. He's having a
relapse of it now. I think we're going to need emergency surgery." I
rushed my words out, not even giving much of an explanation. They
all knew I was a board-certified pediatrician, but I was also his mom,
and I was going to have to take a backseat to their care.

"Christ," she hissed and glanced at me. "His pulse is thready." Amy
turned and shouted, "Let's get a gurney now!" Within seconds, Micah
had a gurney, and Dad was laying Noah on the bed. The older orderly
was such a kind, caring man. He gave me a look of compassion as
Amy and Dad wheeled the rolling bed into an exam room.

I shuffled along beside the bed, realizing Noah was just sleeping
now. His lips weren't quite as blue, probably because he was sleeping

peacefully, and the condition wasn't as emergent as it had been at home. But this was still the safest place for him, and I was glad we made the choice to come.

"Who's his doctor?" Amy asked as she parked the gurney in the curtained room and locked the wheels.

"Uh, Dr. Butler," I mumbled. I was thankful Noah was so sleepy and out of it. It was better for him this way. If he were awake, he would be scared and panicking and making things worse. This way, he was at least able to sleep through the scariest parts of triage. I clung to the side of his bed and Mom and Dad hovered at the foot.

"Alright, well Dr. Butler doesn't have privileges at this hospital, Lily." Amy's tone was cautionary and concerned, but it was her job to make sure we got the best care. "We can call and inform him that his patient is here and ask for advice on what he prefers, but our team will have to be the one treating your little guy."

Amy never knew I had a son. This was all news to her, but like the professional she was, she took it in stride. She zipped around the tiny space following procedure as another nurse I didn't know walked in to help. I didn't even respond because I knew all of that was true when I made the decision to bring Noah here instead of Mountain View. I watched them get his IV line in and check his blood pressure. He never even roused once because they were so gentle.

"Can I speak to you out here?" she asked and nodded beyond the curtain.

I didn't want to leave his side, but he was hooked up to all the monitors now and Mom and Dad were with him. So I followed her beyond the curtain into the main emergency corridor. She took a clipboard with some papers clipped to it and a pen from another nurse and handed it to me.

"Here are some consent forms. You know the drill. You need to sign off so we can call in the specialist if needed..." She looked concerned as I scrawled my name on all the forms without even reading them. I knew the drill and I consented to anything they had to do. "Lily, why bring him here when you work at Mountain View? You know their pediatrics department is bigger. And that's where Dr. Butler has privileges."

I handed the clipboard back to her and shook my head. My shame was my own, and I didn't want it to be public. I couldn't tell her I was hiding from Ethan. Besides, I had every confidence in the staff at St. Anne's. I worked with them. I trusted they could do the job well and help me keep my secret a little while longer.

"I just felt like this was home..." My only regret was that I would pay more coming to St. Anne's since things were in-network at Mountain View. But both hospitals were equipped to help and this one afforded me the privacy.

"Alright, but what am I supposed to say to Dr. Butler? He's going to ask me this, you know." She took the paperwork and tucked it under her arm, but before I could respond, someone across the emergency department coded. The alarms and bells went off, and all available staff hurried that way. She frowned and walked away, and I stood there staring as they tore back the curtain.

"Male, sixty-eight years old, cardiac infarction..." One of the nurses was barking out orders, and the ER docs swarmed the scene.

I covered my mouth and felt tears welling up. Noah lay on that bed with his own body frail and weak. If his blood pressure wasn't controlled soon, he could have his own heart attack. It was a risk factor of this condition, and hearing some other patient coding only made me feel terrified that it would happen to him.

I whipped the curtain back and rushed to his side. The other nurse was just placing his pulse oximeter and I almost ran into her. I clung to him, crying softly, and wanted to climb into his bed and curl up around him while he slept. Mom and Dad hugged each other and talked softly, and I felt completely alone. I didn't want to do this alone anymore.

Suddenly, I realized how stupid I had been for keeping Ethan away from Noah, even now. I wanted Ethan here. Mom and Dad were a slight comfort, but there was something missing. Something intimate that a woman doesn't share with her parents. The vulnerability of letting my guard down and having the strength of a man who is in control and able to help make decisions was something I craved. I wanted Ethan here with me to help me through this.

I sat on the side of Noah's bed and brushed a few strands of hair off his forehead. He looked so much like me that even if Ethan saw him, he might only put the pieces together if he did the math. Even then, he might be convinced that I'd had a one-night stand with someone days after I left Denver, or that Noah was premature. He was small for his age. I could have hidden Noah's true parentage from Ethan a while longer and gotten his expertise when it came to the surgery.

But I had been stubborn and afraid. Mom and Dad, even Amy, challenged my decision to bring Noah here because they knew what I had been uncomfortable admitting. Mountain View was the place Noah should have been. Ethan was the one he should have been seeing. Ethan's expertise was in thoracic surgery, though he was now head of diagnostics. He would have been scrubbing in to help Noah already, and I made a choice based on emotion.

It didn't mean St. Anne's couldn't help. I still stood by that. Fixing a hernia was such a common surgery, I knew there were a few good surgeons here who could do it. I tried to reassure myself that every-thing would be okay, but the nagging fear that I was a bad mother for making this choice ate away at my confidence.

When my phone inside my pocket vibrated, I looked at it. Ethan was trying to call me. I sent it straight to voicemail, but before I got it in my pocket again, it was ringing. Frustrated, I started to ignore it again, thinking Ethan had called right back, but I noticed the caller ID was Dr. Butler, not Ethan.

I wasn't ready for his lecture, but I had to answer. "Hello? This is Lily Carter."

"Dr. Carter, this is Dr. Butler. I just got a call from St. Anne's Hospital. Can you confirm that your son Noah is a patient there currently?" His tone was calm, which I appreciated. He wasn't one of those types of doctors who thought they were God and could boss patients around.

"Uh, yes. I confirm that. We're in the emergency department. He's had a spike in blood pressure and a decrease in respirations. He's slightly hypoxic." I chewed my lip nervously and watched Noah scrunch his nose. He was dreaming. I prayed it wasn't a bad dream.

"Can I ask you why you decided to take Noah to St. Anne's instead of Mountain View? You know we have the best specialists in the state here." I was already doubting my choice and I felt ashamed of it. I didn't like his question, but he deserved a valid answer.

"I, uh... It was just a matter of personal choice. I know these doctors well and..." It didn't matter how well I knew the staff at St. Anne's or why my ego had gotten in the way. Dr. Butler was going to convince me to take Noah to Mountain View.

"Lily, I am going to request a transfer order. You know the team at Mountain View is the right choice. Is Noah stable right now?"

Dr. Butler was so nice and caring, and I was feeling distraught. What I needed wasn't a strong hand to guide me, though he was being that for me right now. What I needed was the man I was clearly in love with to be my pillar of strength, and I couldn't do that if I continued to keep up the charade that I'd been putting on for years.

"Yes, he's stable." My voice shook as I spoke. Bringing Noah to St. Anne's had wasted time, but at least from this point, he would be surrounded by the medical experts he needed and the technology to help him if complications arose.

"Will you let me send the transfer orders?" he asked, and I sniffled.

All the fight within me was gone. It was inevitable. We were going to end up at Mountain View, and my secret would be exposed, and after carrying this guilt for so long, it almost felt like I was relieved to have it so close to being over with.

"Alright..." I conceded. In the face of the fears I was facing, I knew it was better to admit my poor choice and be willing to humble myself than to continue lying and hope I didn't get caught. "I'll sign the orders when they come through. I just need Noah to be in the hospital and have this surgery now. I know you wanted his vitals under better control, but we can't wait any longer."

"No problem. I'll call the best thoracic surgeon we have at the View and we'll have things set up for as soon as he's cleared through preop." Dr. Butler hung up before I could say another word, and I sniffled again.

It would be better if Ethan heard it from me that we had a son, that I'd hidden things from him. I knew him. He wouldn't be upset at all that I never told him I had a son. His anger or hurt and betrayal would come when he learned the child was his. When that happened, all bets were off as to how he would react or whether he would choose to treat Noah.

Ethan was the best, but even the best can make mistakes. The emotion of this situation could cause him to make mistakes, which was why it was illegal for him to perform this surgery. But if I knew him, he would take the case. He'd want to do everything in his power to save our little boy and get him on the path to healing and recovery.

The explosive reaction would come later when he and I were alone and he was forced to confront the fact that I had lied to him. I didn't know if my heart could handle that, not after reconnecting with him. I had tried so hard not to let my heart get so attached, and my fear was being realized. My secret would come out and Ethan would hate me.

I'd be plunged into isolation again, worried I'd never find a man who loved me the way Ethan had. My heart was breaking already and he didn't even know it.

20

ETHAN

I slogged into work feeling a bit discouraged. Lily left after lunch and apparently had shut her phone off. She hadn't returned my calls either, though I didn't blame her. When Dad had the slip and fall and ended up in the hospital, I didn't pay attention to my phone either. Family was more important when things like this happened, and Lily and I, though we were hopefully on a track to be family someday, weren't quite there.

The phone rang off the hook back in the office, nurses rattling off stats of different patients. I was mostly overseeing the team of doctors who were diagnosing patients. Our diagnostic team was one of the very few in the country that were even warranted. With so very few rare conditions, average general practice or attending physicians could handle the bulk of the patient loads in their respective hospitals.

Most of our work came via consultation calls from other hospitals around the country. My team carried around five or six "second opinion" cases every week, and we had partnerships with several major health networks to facilitate serving more sick patients around the country. I really enjoyed the work, though sometimes it was boring and I missed St. Anne's and the surgery department.

After topping off a cup of coffee in the doctor's lounge, I made a pitstop in the men's room and headed to my office. The long day of work was almost over, and I looked forward to the meal stewing in the crock pot on the kitchen counter. I also looked forward to catching up with Lily and seeing how her father was. I hoped that everything was okay and that we could pick up where we left off.

She had stared at the papers with such disbelief I thought she was awestruck over it. I thought it was a romantic gesture to offer them to her, and the tears she shed upon seeing them were happy tears. It was why I kissed her, why we had sex like that. The self-doubt creeping in as I returned to my office, however, had me second-guessing myself. What if she was really going to tell me she wasn't interested and I took advantage of her vulnerability? She had mentioned she wanted to discuss something with me, and I never gave her the chance.

Organizing my files so they were in place for tomorrow's workday, I dialed Lily's number again but it went to voicemail again. I had the thought to swing by her parents' place, but I didn't want to be too forward. If her dad really was ill, a visit from a stranger from Lily's past might not be a welcome thing. I would have to wait until things settled down and she was ready to talk to me.

In the meantime, I had to do my job, and I had to take care of my own aging parents who needed me more than I needed them. I stood, taking my car keys and phone, and headed to the door, but before I got into the hallway, my phone rang. I turned and looked at the desk and rolled my eyes. Technically, I had thirty more minutes left in my shift and after that, all the call-ins would go to Dr. Adams who was on call, but something in my gut told me to answer it.

So I slunk back over to my desk and sat down. Picking up, I answered. "Dr. Matthews, how can I help you?"

"Dr. Matthews, I'm glad I caught you. This is Dr. Butler from pediatrics." The name sounded familiar, but I didn't interact with many doctors in the pediatric wing unless they had a child with a rare condition they needed a consultation for.

"Yes, Dr. Butler. What can I do for you?" I sighed and settled in. It could be a long night if there was trouble with a child, which made my heart ache. Treating adults was difficult at times, but children were so challenging emotionally. I wanted children of my own someday, and watching other people's kids suffer was heart-wrenching.

"Well, we have a young patient, a four-year-old boy with a bad case of diaphragmatic hernia. It's congenital and he's been through one surgery already, which means scar tissue." He paused, and I was already thinking through the steps to diagnosis in my head. If they knew what it was, why did they need me? "The situation is complicated by high blood pressure and difficulty breathing. The child is small for his age, underweight and of smaller stature due to poor digestion and heart complications. We need surgery immediately."

Again, I felt baffled, considering I wasn't in the surgical department, though my degree and expertise were in thoracic surgery.

"Dr. Butler, I can give you the name of a very good surgeon, though he is not typically a pediatric surgeon. He's on call this evening. His name is Dr. George Adams and—"

"With all due respect, Dr. Matthews, you are the best. I don't want just any surgeon working on this child. We need a specialist, a thoracic surgeon with a delicate hand. This boy is frightened of doctors and in very shaky health right now." Dr. Butler sounded certain that this boy needed me, and I knew when one of my peers was so compelled to burden me with their expectations, I needed to listen.

"Alright, let me just stop down for a consultation and see how it goes. If the child is as bad as you say, you can prep an OR and we'll be in surgery in under thirty minutes." I hadn't done a surgery in months, and that was a minor vascular repair for a post-heart-attack patient.

"Perfect, I'll send notice to the OR now." Dr. Butler hung up, and within thirty seconds, I had a text on my cell phone giving me the patient's age, room number, and name.

Noah Carter, age four, pediatrics room 422.

I stared at the information for a second and decided to feel grateful that I could help a little boy feel better instead of being grumpy that it would delay my call to Lily. Mom had food in the crock pot and Dad wasn't going to take visitors tonight anyway, so I sent a message to my neighbor, Mrs. Hensley, to let her know I needed her to pop in and check on Mom because I'd be working late. Then I went to pediatrics to find my patient.

As I walked, I ruminated over the child's name. Noah Carter—it made me smile. I thought of Lily and the coincidence that her last name was Carter also, and then I thought of what we might name our child if we had one. Noah was a nice name. It meant peace and rest from a curse. In Biblical times, Noah was a man of great wisdom and leadership abilities. It was something Lily would probably pick too, her parents being devout Christians.

I waltzed into the pediatrics department with a half-smile on my face and a skip in my step. Just thinking things like that made my heart come alive. Lily and I could have a family. We could be in love and be married. Mom and Dad could finally have grandchildren, and my irrational fears of growing old alone and not having anyone to care for me would go away.

"Dr. Matthews?" I heard, and I turned toward the nurses' station to see an older middle-aged doctor with a patient file in hand looking up at me.

"Dr. Butler?" I asked, and he nodded in acknowledgement, so I walked in his direction.

"I have the patient's file here." He handed it to me, and I folded it open and started looking through the notes. Things were as they seemed, diagnosed with congenital diaphragmatic hernia in utero and surgery already before he was a year old.

"Are the parents aware that the boy needs another surgery?" I asked and folded the file shut. I would need an MRI to confirm how bad this was if it hadn't already been ordered.

"She is," he said firmly.

"She is? No Dad?"

"None listed," Dr. Butler grunted and continued. "I can show you to the room and introduce you. I have the CT and MRI results up in the radiology review room too. When we are done briefing the family, we'll go there so you can prepare your plan for surgery."

He led and I followed. We chatted about the boy's medical past previous to this, and I agreed that with his blood pressure a little unstable, waiting a week or two for new medications to control it was a good idea, given the hernia didn't seem too dangerous. Now we were at the point it had to be done, and I was glad they called me. This would be a touchy surgery.

When he opened the door and pulled back the curtain, however, I was shocked. No—shocked didn't begin to touch what I was. Horrified? Dumbstruck? Sick to my stomach?

Lily sat in a chair next to the bedside of the little boy who was so pale he looked like a ghost. I walked in and stood at the foot of his bed and studied his perfect face. Dimpled chin like hers, thin, petite lips, a mop of brown chestnut curls all identical to his mother, who held his hand, kissing it as he slept.

"Dr. Matthews, this is Lilian Carter, M.D. She's a pediatrician here at Mountain View, and this is her little boy, Noah." Dr. Butler gestured, but I was so speechless I couldn't even fumble out a greeting.

Lily's Mother stood in the corner of the room too, watching, mouth covered by a hand. I didn't see her father, but my vision was blurred, affected by the physical symptoms of shock. Four-year-old son? She was gone for almost five years. That's four years to be alive and almost one year of pregnancy... Could this be...?

"Dr. Matthews?" Dr. Butler said, and I blinked hard and snapped out of it.

"Uh, yes. Dr. Carter." I nodded at her and then opened the file, trying to focus on anything but the million questions in my head. "Tell me what happened to escalate the hernia." I wanted to handle this professionally, but my heart was hammering against my ribcage. Lily had a son she never told me about?

"Well, he was napping and I left home to stop by a friend's house..." Her voice trailed off for a second, and my gaze met hers. I saw the sparkle of tears in her eyes and knew I was that friend whose house she visited. "He woke up and Mom was watching him. He never told her he was awake. He jumped on the bed, and Mom found him and scolded him, but the damage was done."

She looked terrified, and I felt terrified for her. I also felt selfish for

SILVER FOX'S SECRET BABY

having the feelings I was having in the wake of such a huge situation for her. I loved her. I had to focus.

"And what did you experience since that point?"

Lily began to explain every symptom Noah had exhibited since and how they went to St. Anne's. I questioned in my head why she went there, but there was no reason. Nothing made sense. They were a smaller, less-well-equipped hospital. She had to have been hiding something, or someone, from me. That was why she didn't want him to come here. She didn't want me to see him.

Getting through the consultation challenged me to my core, but I made it. I felt like my face tone probably matched the sick boy in bed, who might be my son. I was upset and anxious, probably pale. I asked all the questions I could think I might need to know answers to and then excused myself with a promise to meet Dr. Butler in the radiology review room.

I had to get out of the room and breathe. I needed to put distance between me and Lily. The way I was feeling was not conducive to a safe surgery. My emotions were too heightened, too overwhelming to do this alone. I stepped into the hallway and paged Dr. Adams who I knew very well could also perform this, though he might want advice. We'd have to do it as a team, because if my gut was right, it wasn't even legal for me to operate on that little boy.

Dr. Adams responded with an affirmative and gave me a five-minute window to try to relax. I stepped around the corner and ran a hand through my hair and took a deep breath. The boy looked like her, not me. There was no evidence that he was mine. It was very possible that after I hurt her, she ran off and had rebound sex and wound up pregnant. We were usually very careful, though we did have a few times we thought we might have been irresponsible. But she would have told me, right?

I pressed my eyes closed and leaned my head against the wall. She would have told me. I kept repeating the words in my head over and over, trying to convince myself that the woman I loved would never have lied to me about something so important.

"Ethan, can we talk?"

I opened my eyes to see Lily standing there wringing her hands. She looked terrified, but with what was going on with her little boy, she had plenty of reason to be. I wanted to wrap my arms around her and comfort her, help ease the uncertainty and pain she was having. But I saw hesitancy too, as if she was afraid of me for some reason. As Noah's surgeon, I had to talk to her. I just didn't know if I wanted to talk about the topic she had in mind.

"Of course," I told her, standing straighter. I pushed off the wall and straightened my tie—the tie she tore off me only a few hours ago.

"Ethan, I've been meaning to tell you since I got back. We had so many times I wanted to say something, and I just got panicked and I couldn't say it. You were so amazing and loving, and I didn't want you to be upset with me." Her lip quivered and she blinked out a few tears.

"Why would I be upset? So you had a child and didn't tell me. We are just getting to know each other again, Lily." I resisted the urge to take her hand because all of those words were my own self-reassurance. I was trying to convince myself this wasn't happening because the more she spoke, the more I knew what she was going to say.

"I'm not sure you understand fully." She audibly whimpered and continued. "Ethan, Noah isn't just my little boy."

"Please, Lily..." I willed her not to say it, not to put that in my mind before the most important surgery of my life.

"I have to, Ethan. You have to know. I need you to know and I need you to understand. I never meant to hurt you." She started sobbing, and I couldn't take it. My heart broke, and I reached for her, but the elevator doors behind me opened and I knew it was Dr. Adams.

"He's my son?" I asked in a whisper, and she covered her mouth and sobbed harder, and I knew.

"Hey, now, don't you worry." Dr. Adams walked up with confidence and slapped me on the back of the shoulder. "Matthews and I are on the case, Momma. Your little guy is going to be A-okay and we'll get him all patched up." The man had no clue what was going on between us or how hard this would be for me. But I had to do it.

"We have to go get ready, Dr. Carter." My tone was calm and even, but she winced as if I were chastising her. I didn't have time to discuss it further. The OR was booked and we had to review the imaging results before we cut into my little boy's body to hopefully repair it.

"Go on back and be with him while we prepare. We'll come get him when it's time." Dr. Adam's cool bedside manner made Lily scowl, and she retreated and then he turned to me. "Moms, huh? All the emotion." He turned toward the elevators and said, "You coming?"

I stared after her for a moment with no breath in my lungs.

I had a little boy, and now it was my job to save his life.

After that, I could fall apart.

21

LILY

I didn't care what hospital policy was or what the doctors would think. I didn't even care if it affected my job and the hospital administration came into the room. I delicately adjusted all the lines and tubes Noah was hooked to and lay in bed with him, holding him. Dad finally returned from the cafeteria with some food, but I had no appetite. I was too emotional.

"You should really eat, Lily." Mom tried to gently coax me away from Noah, but I wasn't leaving his side until they took him out. He was scared and they had given him something to calm him so he wouldn't get too worked up. So he was drugged and not as responsive as normal, but if he needed me, I'd rather be in bed with him than eating.

"Mommy, I not want to go." The words were void of emotion, but I could tell if he hadn't been slightly sedated, he'd have been crying or panicking. I knew my son too well, and I hated how this made him feel.

I pushed a few of his bangs off his forehead and cupped his cheek, then kissed his forehead. "I know, baby, but you'll be sleeping the whole time. When you wake up, Mommy will be here and you'll feel better."

When he was sick like this, it made me feel so vulnerable. Mothers wear their hearts on their sleeves when it comes to their children. There were just too many things he could possibly suffer for me to stop worrying until he was back in my arms. And even then there were more risks—infection, complication with anesthesia, recurrence again.

Noah closed his eyes with an unhappy look on his face, and I looked up when the door swished open. Dr. Butler walked in, followed by two nurses and another man, the one I'd seen in the hallway with Ethan just after I had told him the truth. I didn't move a muscle. I was firmly planted next to my little boy who needed me. Noah's hands were in fists around my T-shirt, anyway. I'd have had to pry him away just to sit up.

No one gave me a disapproving look, but the two doctors did come stand by my side while the nurses busied themselves around the room. I didn't pay any attention to what they were doing. I knew this was the group come to take Noah down for surgery, and I wondered where Ethan was. He should have been here.

"Dr. Carter, it's time to get Noah ready for the procedure." Neither one of the men wore their white coats, and the nurses had changed from scrubs into street clothes. My heart swelled at the way they showed so much concern for Noah's mental wellbeing. Not many places would go to such lengths to help a child feel at ease.

"He's a little scared still, even with the meds." I pushed myself up onto an elbow but remained reclining next to him. "Noah, baby, it's time for you to take a nap for a while, okay? These nice men are going to help you feel better." I knew if I said any words that he knew were related to doctors, he would panic and make his blood pressure go haywire again. It was so important for him to stay calm.

"Okay, Mommy," he croaked, and I saw how drugged he was. He could barely hold his eyes open. One nurse smiled at me as he put a syringe into Noah's IV and injected what I could only imagine was probably a light sedative to increase the sedation for Noah until he saw the anesthesiologist.

When his eyes were shut tightly, I slipped out of bed and straightened my clothes and hair. Dr. Butler gestured to the other doctor. "This is Dr. Adams. He'll be working with Dr. Matthews to perform the surgery. The two of them will readjust the position of Noah's organs that have been displaced by the hernia, the stomach and parts of the small intestine, and then they will repair the hernia in the diaphragm."

Dr. Adams stretched out his hand and said, "He's in good hands, Momma. Dr. Matthews and I will take the best care of him."

I shook his hand but I was confused. "Isn't Dr. Matthews going to come and brief me on the surgery?"

"That's why I'm here. Matthews is already in the scrub room getting ready to go into the OR. What we'll do is..." His voice droned on as he explained the delicate procedure and exactly how they would make the incisions and repair the damage.

My mind was scattered, though, remembering the look on Ethan's face when I told him Noah belonged to him. The shock and pain in his eyes seared my conscience, doubling the agony I was in. I didn't want to sit around feeling sorry for myself because that wouldn't help anyone, but I felt like a hiker with a broken leg. I just wanted my hiking party to stop so I could sit and rest for a minute. The pain was too much to handle.

I crossed one arm over my belly and rested my elbow on it, covering my mouth. I was sure every parent whose child was going into surgery felt similar feelings, but I doubted very much that their hearts were also dealing with something like this at the same time. I was exhausted. I wished they had a drug that could knock me out for about a week so I could just wait for the worst to pass and wake up when I felt more emotionally capable of handling things.

"So we'll be in there between three and four hours," Dr. Adams continued, and I came back to the reality that my little boy was about to be cut open. "He'll go straight to ICU when he's done, which means no Grandma and Grandpa in there. But hopefully, he'll only be in ICU for eight to twelve hours before he gets his own room. From there, Dr. Butler can keep us updated on his condition."

"Uh, thank you," I managed to squeak out, and Dr. Adams nodded.

I didn't know him at all, but if Ethan called him in to help, I had to trust him.

"No problem. We'll get to the OR and get started." His smile wasn't warm enough to melt my terrified heart. I backed away as the nurses and Dr. Butler unlocked the wheels of Noah's bed and hung his IV bags on new hooks, now attached to the bed. They pushed the large bed out the door and into the hallway, and the room suddenly felt empty.

Dad came and stood by my side with his hand on my back, and I leaned my head onto his shoulder and let a tear escape as we watched them maneuver Noah and shut the door, and when he was gone, I turned into Dad's strong arms and cried into his chest.

"Come sit down on the couch, sweetheart." Dad's strong arms guided me toward the hard vinyl pull-out sofa Mom sat on. It would be my bed for the next several days, or one like it, anyway, while Noah was recovering. For now, it was where we were waiting for the doctors to repair the hernia and bring him back to me.

"He's going to be okay." Mom took my hand, and Dad sat on the opposite side of me. "The doctors know what they're doing." Her soft touch was comforting.

"Thanks, Mom." She was trying. That was all that mattered. She just had no idea the depths of my misery, being locked inside my head with the thoughts of my little boy on an operating table being supervised by a man who was probably also emotionally distraught. I had to pray that Ethan was capable of separating his personal feelings from the professional task he was doing.

"Did you tell him?" Dad asked gently. He had no idea what had transpired or how Ethan looked when the revelation sank in. It still haunted me. I couldn't get that expression out of my mind. I had done that. I hurt him like that, and there was no taking it back.

"I did." I sighed and leaned back on the couch, feeling dread sit on my chest. "He looked shocked and hurt. He's probably really angry." If my hands were shaking so badly, how would the hands of a surgeon work under the same duress?

"How did he seem to take it?" Mom asked. She angled herself on the couch to face me better, and I closed my eyes and let her hold my hand more tightly.

"He was pretty shocked. I think he was really upset with me, but that other doctor, Dr. Adams, walked up and interrupted us." Adams clearly had no clue what had transpired between us, and if he knew, he'd have forced Ethan to step back and let him handle it all. Colorado state law was clear. Ethan was barred from practicing medicine on people he was related to. It was a means to ensure all patients got the best care and all doctors were levelheaded when treating them.

In this case, the shock alone would make Ethan vulnerable to making mistakes. I knew he was an excellent doctor and surgeon and he was ethical, too. He would stand down if he knew it was going to put Noah at risk.

"Alright, well the only thing we can do is wait for Noah to come back to us now. We'll deal with the other stuff later. Alright, sweetheart?" Dad patted my knee and reached for the Styrofoam container on the table at the end of the sofa. He set it on my lap and opened it, and the smell of the hospital's grilled cheese wafted up to greet me.

"Dad," I groaned, "I'm not hungry."

"Nonsense. You haven't eaten since a little before lunch and it's almost eight now. You'll need your energy for when Noah comes back."

I sat up and readjusted the carryout dish on my lap, and Dad handed Mom one of her own. Hers was a deli sandwich, and she smiled and thanked him warmly, but all I could do was sit there and tear up. The food would be tasteless and it looked even more unappetizing, but that wasn't why I was crying. My heart was so full of emotion, it had nowhere to go and I had to let it out.

"Are you okay, Lily?" Mom asked. She wiped a bit of mayo from the corner of her lip and looked at me with such compassion.

"I ruined everything, Mom." I sobbed and covered my face and felt someone take the food off my lap. Dad pulled me against his chest in his strong arms again and spoke soothing words, but I cut him off. "Dad, please. You don't understand." I pushed him away and swiped at my cheeks. "Ethan was ready to go to HR and tell them we were dating and in love. He told me he wanted me back in his life.

"You know—both of you—how much I loved him. How badly it turned out last time—how hurt I was. He is so amazing and wanted to make it right, and my secret and the way I ran off with his baby and never told him just ruined any chance I had. He'll never love me again. And now my heart..."

The complexity of the past few months of getting reacquainted with him had collided with the past in a cataclysmic explosion that changed the entire direction of my future now. I wanted Ethan. I fell back in love with him, as if I'd ever stopped loving him to begin with. And now I wouldn't have that. I had to mourn him all over again.

"Alright, Lily," Dad sighed. "I think you need to rest. You're getting in your head too much. Do you want me to get you some sleeping tablets?" Mom was already standing as Dad set the grilled cheese on the table. They made space for me to lie down. Maybe a nap before Noah returned wasn't a bad idea. Though I doubted I'd even fall asleep, or if I did, that I'd sleep well.

"No. I'm so emotional I'll have no problem being a zombie for a few hours." I lay down with my head on the arm of the couch, and Dad pulled a blanket from the storage box near the window to cover me.

"We'll come back in a few hours. We'll be here when Noah comes back." He kissed my forehead. "Rest now."

I closed my eyes before they were even out the door, but my heart would never shut off. It was going to hurt for days, or weeks. Maybe months.

22

ETHAN

The hot water scalded my hands as I scrubbed the disinfectant soap into my palms. The initial shock of learning I had a son was still throbbing in my head, making it difficult to think straight. I had overseen the imaging review with Dr. Adams and at the time still intended to do the surgery with him, but seeing how my hands still shook, I knew he would be the one with the scalpel in hand. I would never risk any patient with my emotional state, let alone my own child.

I blindly went through the motions of scrubbing in and making sure I followed all protocols, but I couldn't get past the look on Lily's face when she confessed. She was planning to tell me many times, and I could pinpoint in my memory every single time I believed she'd have done it. The opportunities were there, and each time, I had gotten called away, to care for Mom, to deal with patients.

But she knew years ago. She knew when she left. I pieced that together from the conversation we had earlier today just after our lunch romp in my bedroom. She muttered something about when she left Denver, and I could have sworn she was going to say she knew she was pregnant. She had to have been pregnant then for this to occur. I looked at Noah's charts.

Not only was my son born at thirty-seven weeks with a heart defect, but those thirty-six weeks fell only seven months after she left, meaning she was pregnant for weeks before she left. It meant she knew. It meant she either cheated on me or Noah really was mine, and the fact that she confessed that he was left zero doubt.

She knew she was pregnant when she left and she left anyway. She kept him a secret her whole pregnancy. She never told me when he was born, or that he had a heart condition. She went through bottle feeding and diaper changes, all while harboring him as her little secret. When he had his first surgery, she never reached out, and she finished medical school and her residency and thought she'd move back here and work at a different hospital and still not tell me.

It must've come as a huge shock when I was there that night at her welcome dinner into Mountain View. She must have almost peed her pants. This entire time, she had to have had so much anxiety and fear over what I'd think or what I'd feel. I'd been pursuing her exclusively, begging her to come back to me. How could she live with herself?

My heart oscillated between knowing how badly she had to have been tormenting herself over the whole thing and how angry I was and hurt that she never came to me. I could have helped her all those years. She didn't have to be alone, and she chose being alone over being with me. It not only said something about the amount of pain I had caused her, but also how little she thought of me.

"Are you okay?" Dr. Adams asked, and I noticed he was standing beside me scrubbing in too.

"Uh, yeah, why?" I asked, rinsing my hands.

"Because your hands are almost raw from scrubbing and they're beet red." He scowled and looked down at my hand, and I looked down too.

He was right. My palms were almost bloodied from the way my nails scraped against my skin. I was tired and emotional. My eyes hurt from staring off into space wide open. I needed some eye drops for moisture and sleep to alleviate the emotions.

"I'm fine…" I sighed, but I realized I wasn't fine. He would see that, and I knew I couldn't operate. "But I need you to take lead on this. I'll guide you through, but I can't actually perform the surgery." It was the right call, but I wouldn't hand it over completely. My son needed me, and now, more than ever, I had to be there for him.

Lily had just allowed me to be in his life, and I had to be there. Even if all I could do was stand over the surgeon's skilled hands and guide him in the way he should go, it was what I had to do. Noah deserved the best, and I wasn't the best at this point. My heart was too messed up to do this.

"Of course, Ethan. Is everything okay?" he asked, and he shook the excess water off his hands. It made me wonder exactly how long he had been standing there scrubbing before he said something. Our ritual took at least fifteen minutes to scrub in.

"Yes. It will be fine. I just have some tough decisions to make and I need some time to think about things." If I told him it was in regard to this specific patient and my relationship to him, I would be relegated to the observation room above the theater. My opinion and guidance in this surgery would be rejected and I would be benched. State law was state law. But when it came out later that Noah was my son, and it would have to be proven by paternity tests, I'd just explain I didn't know until after the surgery.

"Alright, well let's get in there and get this rodeo going." He smiled at me just as the nurse entered to help us finish up.

I shook my hands off and let the scrub nurse help me gown up. She laced it on and tied it behind me, then helped Dr. Adams do the same. When she put my mask and gloves on, I thanked her.

The next four hours went exactly as hundreds of other surgeries I had performed over the years, except with me directing the talented hands of another surgeon and not my own. Dr. Adams handled everything with finesse, not skipping a beat. He didn't protest my instruction at all. Whether that was because of my seniority or he just trusted my expertise, I'd never know. We worked as a seamless unit, and once the surgery was underway, I was able to push any thought about Noah being my son aside and do the procedure step by step.

When it was over, I was drained, and so was Dr. Adams. I had been on the clock for more than sixteen hours. His exhaustion came from the intense focus it takes to perform an operation like that for that long of time without losing concentration. I asked him, being the on-call doctor, to do the follow-up with the family, and I scrubbed out and left the hospital.

I had missed dinner and helping Mom to bed. I knew the neighbor was there, so I felt at ease. I'd explain to her in the morning what happened. I just didn't want to go home. Despite my fatigue, I drove for a while, just taking in the city lights after midnight, and I realized I didn't want to be alone. I needed company, and the only person I could think of who might still be awake this time of night was my night-owl of a father.

So I drove to the nursing home and walked through the front doors and up to the nurse's desk. The night watch nurse smiled at me with familiarity. I hadn't visited Dad in the middle of the night in ages, not because of his fall and broken hip, but because I could no longer afford the lack of sleep. Lily's presence in my life had made me hyper-aware of how little sleep I'd gotten because I spent my waking hours thinking of her or trying to be with her.

"Hey, Dr. Matthews, your dad is actually awake." She stood and nodded down the hallway. "We just had to give him some pain meds, but he should still be aware enough for a visit. Do you want the book?"

The book to which she referred was a novel I had been reading to him when I did visit. We were about halfway through, though I never got more than a chapter read before he dozed off. Tonight was not a novel night. It was a night for companionship and male bonding, if he wasn't in too much pain or too grumpy.

"Not tonight, thank you. I'll just let myself in." I smiled and nodded at her, then yawned as I turned up the hallway. The light in his room was on, fingers of it stretching beneath the cracked door. I pushed it open and walked in, and he turned over his shoulder with a glower.

"I told you not to leave the door open, you—Oh, Ethan. I didn't know it was you. come on in." I could see pain etched on his face. The blankets were pulled up over his body, but the way he lay on his side, I could see the thick outline of bandages on his hip.

"I just thought I'd stop by for a visit. You look unhappy. Are you in a lot of pain?" Mom and I had been in and out, but most of the time, he was sleeping or drugged. I heard from his physical therapist that he was fighting them, resisting getting out of bed.

"You have your guts cut open and see how happy you are." He turned back toward the glowing TV screen that displayed the nightly news. I walked over and sat down on the far side of his bed in the chair normally reserved for Mom. "These idiots have no clue what they're doing. They call this politics and it looks more like a circus." Dad scoffed and used the remote to shut the TV off.

"Yeah..." I sighed, not really following what was going on in the world recently. My heart was too thrilled and elated to think of anything but the woman I loved for so long that this punch to the gut was a shocker. Now I just wanted answers and for someone to stop the pain.

"What's eating you? You're looking old and tired. That's my job." Dad winced and let out a yelp as he turned onto his back and used the remote to begin raising the head of his bed.

I didn't disagree with him. I hadn't seen a reflection of my current appearance, but my inward thoughts and emotions were definitely that of someone who was tired, worn out, and haggard.

"Well, I got some shocking news today and it's taken the wind out of my sails." I loosened my tie and rubbed my tired face. "I just can't..."

"Can't what? You're a man. Deal with it, Son. That's what men do." His old-fashioned masculinity was called for at times. There were times when men just needed to be men and take care of things, but then there were times when the rug got swept out from under them and they needed a little stability. This was one of those times.

"Dad, you're a grandfather." I didn't stop to think whether Lily would want me telling my parents. I needed advice and he was it for me. Besides, how would he ever fathom what I was going through unless I gave him the truth?

"What do you mean?" He looked confused and narrowed his eyes at me. "You're not even dating someone seriously."

"But I was." I squirmed in the chair and drew my tongue along my teeth beneath my lip, and Dad's scowl returned.

"There's a story behind this?" he asked, and I nodded.

"A long one I don't have time for. Just know that it's official. You're a grandfather, and my heart is broken and I'm not sure how to handle this at all." The details of it all weren't important to me, though I'd have to cough them up at some point. He would want to know what happened, and I just didn't have the emotional capability to discuss it any more tonight.

"How old is he?" Dad asked, and I could barely answer.

"Four."

"So she kept him from you? I'm assuming it was the woman from a few years back who vanished?" Dad knew more to that than Mom did, and I hadn't even told him I was seeing her again. His questions came without responses and he kept talking. "And if your heart is broken, I assume that means you love her. Well, Son, all I can say is, do you think there weren't times in my marriage where I wanted to give up?

"Do you think I was never angry with your mother? Think she never let me down or disappointed me? Let me tell you something about love. People are human. They're going to break your heart. In fact, the only ones who can break your heart are the ones you've trusted with it. And they never mean to break it. They're just the ones you've let be close enough to you that your heart could break by their mistakes.

"People make mistakes all the time, but they don't necessarily affect you because you don't care about them. But when someone you love hurts you, it hurts really badly. But you're human too. And you are going to hurt her. You're going to break her heart and you're going to regret it. Take that with a grain of salt, Son. And maybe you'll feel differently about this situation. Now get out of my room and let me sleep."

I chuckled at his frankness and absorbed all the wisdom he just spat out at me as I stood. "Thanks, Dad, I really needed to hear that."

He struggled with his covers so I pulled them up for him.

"Anytime, Son."

I left feeling a little better about things, but still heartbroken. Dad was right. I was going to let her down as many times as she let me down, and the choice about how I reacted to those heartbreaks was mine to make. I got to decide how I handled this. My emotions didn't.

I wanted to do it right because even though there was hurt there, I still loved her. I still wanted her.

23

LILY

I was still dozing when they rolled Noah's bed back into the room. Mom and Dad sat in the corner in two chairs the nursing staff had brought in, and I sat up with the ruckus. Rubbing my eyes, I stood and walked over to Noah's bed. He looked so helpless and fragile. His body was draped in a gown, though it wasn't tied onto him, and he was covered in blankets to the waist.

"How did he do?" I asked just as Dr. Adams walked into the room. I didn't expect Ethan to come in because he hadn't come before surgery to say anything to me. It took the average amount of time, which I assumed meant no complications.

"He did just fine. He's under light sedation right now, but the general anesthesia is worn off." Dr. Adams wasn't wearing his mask or bonnet, but he still had on his surgical scrubs. "Things were pretty routine. He'll be on pain meds and antibiotics. You know the drill. But I say he will wake up tomorrow feeling hungry. We'll keep him on a soft foods diet for a few days to make sure his intestines are in the right spots and nothing gets backed up."

I breathed a sigh of relief and looked up at his blood pressure reading on the machine mounted to the pole on his bed. It was almost normal, and following surgery like that, it was a good sign.

"Thank you, Dr. Adams." I sighed. "Dr. Matthews didn't want to come speak to me?" The tiny shred of hope I held inside my heart was hanging on by a thread.

"He was exhausted after the surgery and asked me to come speak with you. He worked all day today, so he went home to rest. If you need anything, I'll be on call all night. I'll be here in the hospital, but I'm going to rest. The nurses will keep a close eye on Noah for us, though. You should try to rest too. Do you need anything?" Dr. Adams looked at me and then my parents. I shook my head and sat on the edge of Noah's bed and took his hand.

I didn't even pay attention to when he left or when the nurses let us have the room to ourselves. I felt numb and empty inside. The weight of everything that had happened left me feeling off-kilter and hollow. I wanted more than anything to be able to say something to Ethan to make him understand what I went through, why I had done what I had done. But no words would ever be able to explain the secrecy or why I ran away.

This little boy lying in this big bed was all I had now, and part of me even feared I wouldn't have him much longer. Ethan was wealthy beyond belief. Not only did he have a huge, cushy salary, but he'd been born to money. I came from humble beginnings and at times so far in my life, I had struggled to make ends meet. This job was a step in the right direction, but I was nowhere near where I could be yet.

If Ethan threw his weight—or money—around, I would be looking at a custody lawsuit I wouldn't be able to afford to fight. Not to mention the courts would frown on my keeping Noah a secret for so long, especially with his condition. And Ethan was able to provide much better care for him too, though it wouldn't be me. Now I had a whole host of fears I hadn't had before. Ones I didn't know how to combat alone.

"He looks so little," Mom said, and I felt her hand resting on my back.

"He does." I wanted to cry. I wanted my eyes to open up and drench me with tears that would wash away every emotion I had and make me feel better. But no tears would come. I had cried so much already, I felt like my body was dried up. I was a feather adrift in a desert, waiting to be caught on a rock and wither.

"Do you want me to get you a glass of water?" she asked, but I didn't want water. I wanted Ethan. I wanted the flicker of intimacy we had regained because I felt so hopeless and lost. I wanted him to yell at me and scream and be mad, and then I could beg forgiveness and this whole thing would go away and we could be a family. I wanted what he promised me before he learned what a horrible person I was.

"No, but I do want my phone." My eyes stayed fixed on Noah's face, watching him sleep. It wasn't losing Ethan that hurt me. It was the not knowing. How was he feeling? What was his response? Where was he? What was he thinking? Why hadn't he come back and reacted?

Dad handed me my phone which was almost dead. I dialed Ethan's number and held the phone to my ear, but it went straight to voice-mail which wasn't encouraging at all. It was late. I should have just assumed that Dr. Adams was telling the truth, but Ethan had just gotten the shock of his life. How could he go home and just fall asleep? I knew that wasn't what happened. He was somewhere stewing on this, and I felt so nervous about what he would say when he finally surfaced.

"Lily, you need to rest." Dad gently pried the phone from my hand and turned it off, then laid it on the table next to Noah's bed. "You are no good for Noah if you're sitting up worrying about things you can't control. It's difficult, yes, but your first priority is to be a mother, not to worry about other things."

My gut tied into knots, and I wanted to whimper, but I couldn't even do that. I was a shell of a human being. I couldn't do anything but stare into space and listen to the thrum of my blood rushing past my eardrum.

"Dad's right, baby." Mom pulled my arm and tried to force me off Noah's bed, but I was frozen in place. "You should rest."

"What if he sues for custody?" I asked blankly as I stared at Noah. He hadn't known anyone in his entire life except me and my parents. He barely allowed me to leave him with Kate when she wanted a "fun

141

aunt day." Noah was sensitive and anxious a lot of the time because of his medical traumas, and if Ethan tried to take him, it would cause a huge upset for him.

"Dr. Matthews isn't going to do that to you or his son." Dad was only trying to help, but his bold confidence wasn't based on actual knowledge. He didn't know that at all. And while my heart told me Dad was right, I had been away so long, I didn't even know Ethan as well anymore. He could have changed, or if he hadn't changed that much since we were together, it didn't mean the trauma of learning my secret hadn't changed him.

"Please, let me go," I told Mom, and she loosed my arm.

"At least sit in a chair so you give Noah space to rest." Mom backed away, and when she returned, she had a chair which she planted by the bed. I slid off the mattress into the seat and kept hold of my son's hand.

"We're going to go home and get some rest. We'll come back first thing in the morning. Mom and I aren't young enough to stay up all night the way we used to." Dad's calm tone came with a kiss to the crown of my head and a squeeze to my hand.

"I'll see you in the morning." I didn't even turn to say goodbye. But the moment they were gone, I did pick up my phone and turn it back on.

The door swished shut, and I was already dialing Amber's number. I knew she worked third shift in the diagnostics department. We weren't super close like we used to be, but she reported directly to Ethan. If she had seen him, she would tell me.

"Lily?" she said when she answered. It was late, and I wasn't surprised to hear the shock in her tone.

"Hey, Amber... I have a question."

"Of course... It's late. Is everything okay?" I loved that she cared enough to ask, but I didn't have the energy to explain a whole lot. At least not everything surrounding Noah.

"Uh, yeah, kind of. Have you seen Dr. Matthews tonight?" If he was still in the hospital, I could sneak away from Noah's side long enough to go talk to him. I had to get this off my chest because the fear of not knowing what could happen was killing me.

"No, why? Is everything okay? Do you need me to page him?" She sounded ready, willing, and able to help, but I didn't want her in the middle of it.

"Uh, no... Well, Ethan and I sort of have a relationship going on. Don't worry, he spoke to HR already. We just had a, uh... We disagreed about something, and I just haven't heard from him. I thought he might be down there in diagnostics hiding from me." I forced a nervous chuckle to make her think it was no big deal, but it was a huge deal.

"Ooh, something steamy." She was being playful, and I wanted to cry. "Well, no. I haven't seen him. If I do, I'll tell him you asked. I hope you two work things out. I always thought you'd be cute together."

"Thanks, Amber."

"No problem." She hung up, and I was alone again, only this time, I didn't just feel alone. I knew I was.

This journey life had me on was isolating and cruel. One minute, I thought I'd be okay, and the next, I was bombarded with more than I could handle. My parents didn't fully understand me emotionally, and I had somehow managed to ruin things with the one person who ever had. Tears tried to well up in my eyes, but it was as if I had dehydrated myself to the point my body couldn't even make them.

My eyes burned, my cheeks too. I gritted my teeth and almost screamed, but I didn't want to wake Noah. Instead, I laid my head down on the side of the bed and pressed my eyes shut. There was no point in agonizing over things. I definitely wouldn't sleep, and I would be locked inside my head, but I was still in control of my thoughts.

I decided to think about a plan of action for Noah when we went home, where he would sleep and how I would keep him from romping and busting open his incisions. I had menus to plan and a routine to set with Mom and Dad as far as his childcare and medication schedule. And all of that brought me back around to his custody and whether I needed a lawyer to help me deal with whatever storm awaited on the horizon.

I only knew one thing. I was batting a thousand when it came to my worst days. I had managed to survive them all by putting my face to the wind and setting my gaze on the future. I had to do that now. I just had to do it knowing there might be a war ahead of me. A war I couldn't lose, and one I didn't even want to fight, but if it came to that, I would fight like hell to make sure I won. Nothing was more important to me than my son, not even my own heart—which was already broken and blowing in the wind.

It couldn't get any worse... right?

24

ETHAN

I left the nursing home and started toward home, but the idea of sitting alone in my house while Mom slept felt like torture. I didn't want to be alone anymore. I'd thought that Lily and I had a chance. Now I wasn't sure what we had. She'd been lying to me this entire time. The idea that she could sleep with me and be so intimate and have kept such a huge secret from me had me questioning what was real and what wasn't.

It didn't feel right leaving this hanging in the air. I felt like I wouldn't sleep or be able to work or focus on anything until the two of us had a very long discussion. There were too many things unspoken, so many questions I had about my son and why she never told me about him. And it didn't matter that I knew nothing about him or even what his middle name was. The instant she told me he was mine, love deeper than the ocean welled up inside me for him.

My son had just undergone a major operation and he was lying in a hospital bed weak and probably barely conscious. I needed to be there for him, if for no other reason than to live my life without regret. I didn't know if Lily wanted me there or how she'd react to my wanting to be a part of his life, but I knew if I didn't go, ten years from now, I'd feel like a failure as a father. He was mine, and my heart told me being there for him was the right thing.

So I turned toward Mountain View and decided that if she chased me away, I would at least know that I had tried to be a good father. I know it was what my own father would have done, what my mother would expect me to do. And it eased my heartache the instant I made the decision to do so.

I pulled back into the parking lot a little before two. The place looked like a ghost town. Visiting hours were over at eight p.m. every day, so most family members were already gone for the day. The night shift was light too, not as many doctors and nurses. We didn't do surgeries at night unless they were emergencies, and none of the in-house offices took appointments after five p.m. I was able to park in the front row.

On my way to the elevators, I passed Lily's parents. I met them more than once in the past. They were good people, and I fully believed that Lily had either sworn them to secrecy about Noah or that they had no clue he was mine. I knew they liked me when Lily and I were dating. Though, with as hurt as she was when she left Denver five years ago, it was possible her father harbored a grudge.

"Mr. and Mrs. Carter," I said, approaching them.

They looked uncertain and hesitant. Mr. Carter had a furrow between his eyebrows that mirrored the grand canyon, snaking down his forehead to his aquiline nose. I could see the fatigue in both of their eyes, but Mrs. Carter held a tired smile and her hand shot out to take mine.

"Ethan, it's so good to see you." Her grip was timid and gentle, and I noticed Lily's father did not extend the same gesture of goodwill.

"Ethan," he grunted and placed a protective hand in the small of his wife's back.

"I, uh..." I sighed and then took a deep, calming breath. "Is Lily still up there?" I didn't want them to think I was going on the offensive. Yes, I was very hurt by her revelation, but that talk with my father showed me how human I was, how prone to failure. Lily had been hurt pretty badly. I totally understood her leaving town without saying a word. Keeping the secret once she got back was what hurt me.

"She is," Mr. Carter said, and the frustration in his tone was obvious. "They're resting."

"Did Noah wake up yet?" I figured Dr. Adams had the boy sedated, but there was a chance they had been able to say hello, at least.

"Sleeping," Mrs. Carter said, and she elbowed her husband gently in the side.

I knew any words I had to say to them would fall short of the deep apology I knew they expected. I broke their little girl's heart so long ago, and they were there to pick up the pieces. I left the mess they cleaned up, but I never even realized what a mess that was until it was too late. Until Lily just never returned my calls or showed up. Months went by, not a call or text, and then I heard she left town and gave up hope.

"I know you probably don't know what to say to me or how to act. I want to apologize for what happened five years ago. I don't fully understand Lily's pain, but I recognize how badly I hurt her." My words felt empty, like they were too little consolation a bit too late, but it was all I had to offer them. "I can see why she was upset enough to keep such a secret from me." I assumed they knew what I was talking about and got the confirmation I needed in the recognition on Mrs. Carter's face.

"Ethan, you don't have to—"

"But I do," I said, cutting her off. "I want you to know, Mr. and Mrs. Carter, that I in no way intend to cause problems for Lily or Noah. We have a lot of things to talk about, and maybe it will or out or maybe it won't. But right now, nothing could be more important to me than making sure my son is cared for in the best way possible. That includes making sure his mother is okay."

David's expression softened, and I saw the heart of a father in his eyes. He wanted to make sure his child and grandchild were safe, but my words were bringing him hope. His shoulders relaxed, and he extended his hand to me.

"Dr. Matthews, I appreciate your words and respect your

thoughts." His lips pressed together into a line as he shook my hand, and when he pulled his hand back, he said, "Just make sure she sleeps a little. She's going to be so tired tomorrow when Noah needs her."

I took that as permission for me to go up to their room, which I didn't need, but I valued deeply. I nodded at them, and without saying anything else, Ellen hugged me and then they walked away. I watched them until they walked through the exit doors and vanished into the night. Then I turned toward the elevators.

When I finally walked into Noah's room, I heard Lily snoring softly. She was draped over the side of the bed with her hands wrapped around Noah's. I didn't want to disrupt her, so I shooed the nurses away and checked Noah's vitals myself. His blood pressure and heart rate were steady. He didn't have a fever, and he was resting peacefully.

It allowed me to really take a good look at him for the first time. In surgery, I hadn't allowed myself to really examine him. I had to focus, to keep my heart in check and make sure he got the best care possible. But now, as tears welled up in my eyes, I marveled over how perfect he was. He looked so much like his mother that had she not told me the truth, I would fully have believed her if she'd lied and said he wasn't mine.

He snored lightly too, sounded just like Lily, and I pinched the bridge of my nose to stop from crying. How many years I had lost with him, missing his first steps, first words. I didn't know what his favorite food was or what shows he liked to watch. I wondered if he knew his letters and numbers yet, or if Lily had taught him any nursery rhymes. I wanted to hold him too and cradle his frail little body in my arms to protect him.

So very many emotions washed over me, so many things I wanted to say and ask. But Mr. Carter was right. Lily needed her sleep or she would be no good for him, and since Noah knew nothing about me, I couldn't exactly pick up the slack. Though, just looking at him and how full my heart felt knowing he was mine, I hoped one day, I would be able to. How would that go, anyway? How did you tell a four-year-old, "This man is your father but you've never met him."

I checked his chart as a distraction to avoid crying anymore. This time, I really examined it. The information in my file was limited, but this file on the computer in his room held all his medical records back to birth. Dr. Butler had them forwarded here so that Dr. Adams and I could review them. Noah had been through so much for such a little guy, and I hated that I wasn't there for any of it. I wasn't angry with Lily as much as I was disappointed that I had missed it.

When I locked the computer, I decided to sit down next to her and wait for her to wake up. Certainly, it wouldn't be very long. With her neck craned like that, she'd get a kink in one of those muscles and her body would rouse her. So I pulled up a chair and sat down, but the noise startled her and just as I was seated, she sat straight up and looked at me with surprise and fear.

When the initial shock of being woken up wore off, she said, "Ethan…" and I heard the sorrow in her tone.

"Can we talk?" I asked, nervous she was about to throw me out, but she bit her lower lip and nodded her head.

Now, if God would only grant me the serenity to know the things I couldn't change and the courage to embrace the present, everything would go well.

25

LILY

I rubbed my eyes and stared at Ethan who looked calm, not angry the way I expected. I never heard him come in, and I wondered how long he'd been sitting here watching me sleep. My phone, lying on the mattress by Noah who was fast asleep, was dead. I didn't know what time it was or how long I had been sleeping. My neck hurt, and even though I had been so eager to speak with him and find out how angry he was with me, I suddenly didn't want him in the room.

I felt self-conscious and nervous. I was afraid there would be shouting that would wake Noah, or that I would break down crying and when Noah woke up, he would be scared or uneasy with that. Add to that my fears of Ethan taking Noah away from me, and I was a bundle of nerves and wished Mom and Dad were here to be a shield between me and Ethan.

"Can we talk?" he asked, and I froze.

All of the questions I had earlier this evening were suddenly just out of reach. The things that had been on the tip of my tongue were gone. I couldn't conjure up a single thought other than the gripping fear of losing my little boy and the man I loved all in the same hard conversation. I dug deep and reached for any answer other than "yes", but instead of fight or flight, I found myself like a deer in headlights wishing the car would just hit me and put me out of my misery.

"Lily, I'm sorry."

Ethan's apology wasn't at all what I expected. I thought he'd demand the truth and question me with a thousand things—where I was, how I never told him, what I thought I was going to do for the rest of Noah's life. The words were almost painful because I assumed he was angry with me and would shout or judge me harshly for my mistake. Why was he apologizing to me? I was the one who hurt him this time.

"What?" I mumbled, and then I rubbed my eyes. It had been a long day. For all I knew, this was just a horrible dream and I would wake up to find out what I actually feared happening was true.

"I said, I'm sorry." He looked over at Noah and sighed. Then he continued. "I guess I never really understood how much I hurt you five years ago." Ethan's shoulders dropped as he watched our son sleeping in the hospital bed that seemed to swallow his thin little body.

"I know I apologized for it before, but all of this" —he gestured with his hand— "just shows me how much pain you were in. I know you would never have kept our little boy a secret." He turned to look at me. "It must have destroyed you when I said those words."

My mind had replayed that sentence over and over in my head. When I finally came to terms with the fact that Ethan hadn't called me a mistake but that he'd called our not telling HR early on in the relationship a mistake, it was too late. I was a mother with a very sick child alone in a strange city, and Ethan was for all intents and purposes a stranger to me again.

His hand reached for Noah's arm, and he rubbed his thumb up and down beside the IV port. I could see the pain and fear in his eyes. Pain because of what I'd put him through, and probably fear over how Noah would recover. Or maybe he was worried I wouldn't let him be around Noah, which couldn't be further from the truth. I wanted

Noah to know Ethan. I just wasn't sure how to make that happen with the challenges we faced.

"Ethan, I..." I didn't know where to begin. Nothing I could say would give him back the four years he'd missed with his son. It felt useless saying anything, or even apologizing.

I watched him for a few minutes. He seemed torn, like he wanted to shout at me but knew better. Or maybe he wished I would yell at him, let off all the steam of five years of being alone, being pregnant without him, raising a very sick child who'd been through medical procedures and trauma. I didn't know how to read him anymore. I didn't know if I ever knew how to read him. If I had, maybe we wouldn't be in this situation at all.

"I'm angry with you, Lily." HIs calm statement made me feel ashamed. He had every right to be furious and lash out, but somehow, saying it calmly hurt worse. "You left Denver and you knew you were going to have my baby, but you said nothing. I can't blame you for being upset at me, but I'm hurt that you didn't say anything about Noah."

"Ethan, please, I—"

"Let me finish, please," he said and he turned to look me in the eyes. I saw his emotion there, beneath the surface. He was upset and hurt, but he was controlling all of that in a masterful way. "I'm not angry you left without telling me or that you tried to do it on your own for so long. I believe something inside you knew you couldn't do it alone, and that's why out of all the jobs in this country you could have taken, you chose to return to Denver. You wanted me to know."

My gut churned. Deep down, I knew he was right. I could have chosen to stay at Princeton Plainsboro. I could have taken a job in California, or one in Michigan. And while any of them made sense and I had rejected all of them ultimately because I wanted Noah near his Nana and Pop, the true reason I wanted to come home was because I knew I'd have to tell Ethan. Noah needed his father in his life.

"What I'm angry about is why you didn't tell me as soon as you saw me again. Why let me get so emotionally invested in you and dream of a future with the two of us when you had this secret?" His eyes searched me, and I had to look away.

This was the question I had asked myself a billion times in the past few months. Why had I hidden Noah? Not Noah the fetus in my womb, or Noah the toddler who was sick and needing medical care. But Noah, the four-year-old boy who was such a huge part of my life, who needed his father? The only answer was shame and fear.

"I came back, and I knew eventually, I'd bump into you. I never expected it to be my first day of work at the welcome dinner. I thought you'd still be at St. Anne's or maybe you'd have moved away..." I sniffled and realized I was crying. "You were so amazing, Ethan. I mean, I knew I had this secret and I wanted to tell you so badly, but you were so eager to reconnect and fix things. Every time I wanted to bring it up, we got interrupted by something. A few times, it was like you didn't want to hear what I was going to say."

"I thought you were going to push me away." He frowned and hung his head. The wavy locks I used to run my fingers through were streaked with gray now.

"I thought you'd be angry with me—knew you would." I sighed and rubbed my face, hoping to relax, but until this conversation was over, I knew there would be no relief. "Then I rationalized that I had to wait until this episode with Noah was over. He will be so shocked to learn you're his father, and with the surgery and everything, I just want him to be okay."

"That's all I want too, Lily. Believe me."

I did believe him. I just didn't know how to handle this or how to move forward now. I was stuck in what could have been and not looking forward to what would be. It wasn't like I could snap my fingers and make all my fears and insecurities go away, and I was sure Ethan had his own fears and insecurities too.

"We have a long road ahead of us," he said, and I was confused.

"What do you mean?"

He looked me in the eye and reached for my hand, which I allowed him to take. It felt awkward, like I was waiting to be let down. But I held his hand and his gaze as he continued. "I'm really hurt and angry, but I'm willing to work through all of this if you are. I had a long talk with my father tonight, and he clued me in on some wisdom I don't think I'd ever have come to on my own. At least not in a way that would have preserved the love we have for each other."

A nurse walked into the room, and I looked up at her. Ethan waved her off, and I suddenly felt overwhelmed. My eyes welled up with tears at his words. Work things out?

"You're going to make me angry a million more times in life. You're going to fail me and break my heart and let me down. You're going to hurt me and we're going to argue, because you're human and I'm a human and I'll do all those things to you." His hands were so gentle with mine, cradling them and bringing my fingers to his lips to kiss, one at a time.

I cried harder, tears of relief, tears of guilt and shame. Never did I expect this sort of reaction from him. Awestruck, all I could do was sob and let him cup my cheek with his free hand.

"Lilian Carter, I am in love with you and nothing you can say or do will ever stop that feeling. If being apart for five years never killed the dying embers, how could this? You might have kept it a secret for a while, but you gave me the best gift any man could ever have." Ethan blinked, and a tear rolled down his cheek. He held my gaze with such strength and passion in his eyes, I couldn't look away.

"Please forgive me, Ethan. You have no idea how long I've been torturing myself for this. Noah needs you. I need you..." My voice cracked several times, but I managed to get the sentence out. I didn't deserve his forgiveness, though he had mine. I knew now after all of this exactly what a scared and insecure heart would do to self-sabotage.

When he made the comment about my being a mistake, he was acting in self-preservation. He didn't mean it. I could see now how badly he regretted that and wished it had never happened. I felt the same way. I acted stupidly in my own self-interest at the time, and now I felt horrible for the choices I'd made.

"I forgive you, Lily, and I love you. And I never want us to have secrets again. I'm sorry if it takes me a while to loosen up and let go of this. I ask you to be patient with me for a while as I adjust to it all. I'm sorry if I have insecurities or if I mistrust you at times as I heal and try to sort through all the emotions I'm feeling, but I want you to know I'm fighting for us. Because I believe we have a future together, and while I don't know what it looks like yet, I want it. Know that I really, desperately want it."

Ethan leaned forward and kissed me lightly, and I let him. I kissed him back, finally feeling the weight lift off my chest. I never expected this to happen, though at times, I hoped against hope that it would. Here we were, weeping together with a desire to make things right instead of fighting and running away. There couldn't have been a better resolution to this entire situation, for us and for Noah.

"How will we tell him?" I asked, leaning my forehead on his. The thought hadn't even occurred to me yet, considering I feared the worst for the most part.

Ethan sucked in a breath and squeezed my hand before sitting back. "I think we start slowly. I'll be around more. If he asks, we'll tell him I'm your friend. He's little enough that he probably won't remember a lot of this, and given his fear of doctors, there's a good chance he'll remember almost nothing of these early years.

"We don't have to tell him it all right away. Let him figure it out for himself. I want him to call me Daddy, but we'll give him time to adjust." He turned to me with an abrupt need in his expression and said, "But I want you to know I will never take him from you, even if this doesn't work out between us for whatever reason. I could never do that to you."

Part of me felt guilty again, that Ethan had experienced the pain of having his son hidden from him. How horrible that must've felt for him. But they were together now.

"I love you, Ethan. I'm not sure I ever stopped. I tried to." I chuckled and wiped my face. "My God, did I try to hate you and be angry, but I just couldn't. You have always had my heart."

"Let's work it out, then. Okay?" He put his hand under my chin and kissed me again, and I threw my arms around his neck.

"Yes. I want that more than anything."

This conversation didn't go at all how I thought it might, and for that I was grateful. We had so much to talk about still and work through, but I believed we would make it. If the worst of it was past and we still wanted each other, there wasn't anything we couldn't get through.

156

2 6

ETHAN

Nostalgia hit me the minute I walked through the door into the Carter residence. I had only been here a few times to have dinner with Lily's parents, but those were fond memories I cherished now. David and Ellen were such kind people. It was no wonder Lily turned out as amazing as she had.

"You can just set that stuff over there," David told me, nodding in the general direction of the dining table at the far end of the open space.

I carried a duffle bag with Lily and Noah's clothing, a plastic sack of their things from the hospital, and a vase of flowers one of her aunts had sent to the room for Noah. Ellen followed me through the door with an arm full of teddy bears and a few other small tchotchkes Noah's visitors had brought. It wasn't a dull week by any means.

I spent the majority of my time working like normal, and my evenings were filled with caring for Mom, who had finally recovered from her cold, and shuttling her to and from the nursing home to be with Dad, who was less grumpy now. But every night, I slept in Noah's room on the pullout sofa, giving Lily a chance to go home and shower and rest before returning at first light. It was an exhausting schedule for us both, but it was worth it.

"Here, Ethan," Ellen said, taking the flowers. "I'll go put some fresh water in this. You go help Lily with the boy." She smiled at me and took the flowers as I set the bags down. When I turned to the door, I saw Lily carrying Noah in her arms. If I didn't know he was four, I'd never have guessed it. The congenital condition had really repressed his body's ability to absorb nutrients and stunted his growth, but hopefully, all of that was behind us for the foreseeable future.

"Want me to carry him?" I asked, approaching Lily. She gladly handed him over, and he clung to me. He weighed almost nothing and felt light as a feather, but when his little arms wrapped around my shoulders, I almost melted. Nothing in the world felt better than this.

"So where do you want to sit, buddy?" I asked him, and he pointed at David, who had sat down in the recliner at the end of the coffee table.

"Pop," Noah grunted, and then laid his head on my shoulder. He was recovering well but still very weak and still in pain. It would linger a while, but hopefully, not long.

"Pop it is," I told him and carried him over to sit on Lily's father's lap. The burly man embraced his grandson and started rocking as soon as Noah was settled.

We told Noah this week that I was his mom's friend, that I'd be around for a while. Noah took to me instantly, and when he was awake and feeling okay, he had a lot of questions about monster trucks and sharks, and anything else his four-year-old brain could think of. I soaked up every second of the attention that I could but managed to encourage him to sleep at night when he really wanted to be talking to me.

"I, uh… I should go, I guess." I stood next to Lily and waited for her to acknowledge me. She was hunched over, stacking her dad's magazines on the coffee table to make room for Noah's blood pressure cuff and medications. When she straightened, she had a curious, hopeful expression.

"I was hoping you'd stay for dinner." Her eyebrows rose, and she glanced at her mother, who brought the vase of flowers and placed it next to the stack of magazines. "Mom?"

"Oh yes, dear. Ethan is welcome to stay. I have a roast in the oven that should be ready any minute. It's been cooking all day. And let's see, we'll have apple crisp and vegetables, and—"

"Chocolate pudding!" Noah chimed in, happy to be home. His face lit up like it was Christmas.

"And chocolate pudding for Noah, if he eats all his food." Ellen's eyes sparkled, and I could tell that she loved the boy very much. Being part of this moment and being invited to dinner were priceless to me. I loved how close Lily was with her family and that her parents were young enough to truly enjoy being grandparents. I couldn't wait for my parents to meet Noah someday and feel that same joy.

"Well, if there is chocolate pudding involved, count me in." I winked at Noah, who giggled, and Ellen chuckled. She returned to the kitchen to put finishing touches on our meal, and I helped Lily carry Noah's things to his room and organize them.

The entire afternoon and evening felt surreal. Just a few months ago, I spent my evenings alone with Mom or at the pub after work with coworkers. I had no future in mind other than more caring for my aging parents or building my career up. Now I was looking at a beautiful family of which I desperately wanted to make myself a part. The idea I'd been tossing around in my mind of marrying Lily was slowly becoming more and more concrete by the day, and tonight, I felt like speaking with her father was the next step.

We managed to get everything cleaned and organized, and Lily told me how her parents had been gracious enough to allow them to stay here until she got her own place. But with Noah's illness, she decided it was safer to just stay with them a bit longer, until after his surgery. She'd been letting him stay in her bed with her, but he needed his own space now. It was safer with his incisions to have his own bed. I could tell she was saddened by that fact and that she would rather he continued co-sleeping for a while longer.

At dinner, however, I could tell Noah was excited about the idea of having his own bed. He made a big deal of it too, talking about how he was going to sleep with his toy trucks, which of course, Lily wouldn't allow. He pouted about that, but I loved watching the interaction.

Each little conversation showed me more snippets of his personality and how happy and smart he was. The birth defect might have robbed him of some of his physical vitality, but his mind was sharp.

When he finished eating, he started to doze off right in his seat at the table, so Lily stood and roused him from his slumber. "Time for bed, baby. I'll get your bandage changed and get you your medicine, and then Ethan can tuck you in with me."

I smiled at the sentiment. "I can help with bandages and medicine too," I offered, but she shook her head.

"It's okay. Finish eating. I'll get him ready, and you can say goodnight."

I felt bad allowing her to do all the work, but it did afford me the perfect opportunity to speak with David and Ellen alone. I put my last bite of roast in my mouth and chewed thoughtfully while she collected Noah, and when she left the room, I washed the food down with a swig of soda and wiped my mouth.

"Mr. and Mrs. Carter, I'd like to speak to you about something while Lily's not around, if that's okay." My confidence soared as David nodded his head and pushed his empty plate away.

"What do you have on your mind?" he asked before using his tongue to polish his tooth.

It felt awkward seeking his permission to marry his daughter. For the first time, it dawned on me how much older I was than Lily. At forty, I was halfway between David's age and Lily's, and at times, I felt I had more in common with him than her. Like the fact that my back just didn't work the way it used to and sometimes, I felt like my knees were the knees of a seventy-year-old man.

He stared at me with stern eyes while Ellen stood and started stacking dirty dishes up to be carried away.

"Well, sir, I want Lily and Noah to move in with me. I know you have been providing for them both for a while now, though I'm positive Lily pulls her own weight around her. I just feel like if my family is going to be whole, we should be under the same roof." Nerves played at the corner of my mind as I watched his thoughtful expression. He was mulling it over, as if he had any true say in the matter.

Ultimately, the decision would be up to Lily, but I wanted to do things the right way. Asking for David's blessing in this matter was how his generation was raised. It offered him the respect of approving of our relationship for his little girl and made him feel like I could be trusted.

"I see..." He sighed but said nothing else. Ellen eyed him and smiled at me before picking up her stack of dishes.

"Well, I think it's a lovely idea. Noah will love that, and he'll have two doctors around to keep an eye on him. But Nana will still be babysitting. I need my baby time." She winked and walked off, carrying the dishes through the swinging door into the kitchen.

I turned to David and said, "And I want to marry her." The slight uptick of David's eyebrows encouraged me. "I've loved her for years, and when she came back into my life, I knew she was the one. I messed it up before, but I'm never going to mess it up again. I love her, and I want her in my life forever. I want our family to truly be whole."

David nodded again, and this time, he narrowed his eyes at me. "It's about time," he grunted, and I chuckled, which made him smile. "Welcome to the family, Ethan. I'm sure you're going to make her the happiest woman alive."

"Ethan!" I heard from in the distance, and I knew Lily was calling me to tuck Noah in.

"Thank you, sir. I won't let you or her down." I stood and dropped my napkin across my plate, then headed to the stairs.

Every step I took built anticipation inside me. The excitement I felt when I was considering asking her to marry me last week hadn't abated at all. It was like life had been put on pause, and perhaps tonight wasn't the perfect night, but I knew it would be soon. For now, my focus was on making sure I did everything in my power to be the best partner and father I could be.

I walked into Ethan's bedroom and saw him lying on his side, frowning. Lily sat next to him with a hand on his back, rubbing, and I could see the medicine spoon in her hand.

"It's yucky," he moaned and coughed.

"Yes, but it helps you, baby." Lily smiled at me sadly and gestured with her head for me to come closer.

I walked over and crouched next to his bed, and he looked up at me. "Yucky medicine?" I asked.

"I don't like it." He scrunched up his face and made me snicker.

"Yes, I can tell. But here is the good news. You only have to take that a few more times and then you never have to do it again. Plus, it takes away all of your pain so you can sleep better." I tousled his hair, and he huffed.

"I still don't like it." Noah rolled to his back and crossed his arms over his chest, and Lily placed a soft kiss on his forehead.

"Baby, there's something I want to talk to you about," she said, but as she did, she reached for my hand and I got the feeling she was talking about me.

"More medicine?" he asked in a grumpy tone.

"Not at all, something even better." Her eyes were brimming with emotion when she looked at me. "It's actually about your daddy."

Noah turned on his side again and pulled his glasses off his face and folded them up, then handed them to me. "I don't have a daddy," he said, and that broke my heart, but the pain was short-lived.

"But you do have a daddy. You just never got to meet him yet." Lily looked back at her son, and I was patient. My heart hammered against my ribcage, swelling with joy and pride in this moment. I didn't have to ask her to marry me to know she would say yes. If one week into this thing, she was ready to tell our son about me, I knew she was mine.

"Where is he?" Noah asked, and then he narrowed his eyes at me. "Does Ethan know him?"

I chuckled again, and Lily nodded upward with her head. I got the point she was trying to make, and I knelt closer to his bed.

"I know him really well. In fact, I am him. I'm your daddy, Noah." My own tears refused to be held back. I blinked and shed a few, and he looked at me, very confused.

"Ethan is my daddy? But he's your friend." He turned his confusion on Lily, and she smiled and nodded. Tears streamed down her cheeks, and she wiped them away.

"Yes, he's my best friend and he is your daddy. What do you think of that?" It seemed to be a little too much for his four-year-old brain to handle, but he shrugged and winced at the same time.

"I think medicine is yucky. Maybe you can take it." Again, his face screwed up into a hot scowl and had both of us laughing. We spoke for a few minutes about the idea of my being his father, but I could tell he was sleepy.

When Lily and I left his room with the baby monitor in hand, she took me by the hand and led me downstairs. Ellen and David had retired for the evening, but after the week Lily had, I didn't want to stay and keep her up. She needed to rest while Noah was resting. So, I guided her to the door and asked, "Walk me to my car?"

"Of course." She followed me into the cool night air. It was dark already, streetlights coming on down the street already. The row of hedges next to the driveway shrouded my little sedan in darkness, which allowed me to kiss my beautiful girlfriend in privacy.

"Thank you for everything, Ethan. You've been so amazing, I don't even know how to thank you enough." Her head rested on my chest, and she wrapped her arms around me. I held her against me, careful not to touch any of the buttons on the monitor now clipped to her waistband. "This evening has been so perfect."

"I wish I could stay with you or that you could come to my place." I pulled her harder against myself and ground my pelvis into her thigh, leaving no room for misinterpretation of what I was trying to say.

She snickered and said, "I wish so too, but you know..." Lily glanced around mischievously and then kissed me again. "It doesn't mean we can't sneak around like we're kids again." Her hand rested on the door handle to the backseat of my car, and I felt a thrill of excitement shoot through me.

"Dr. Carter, you're making me blush." I backed away as she pulled the door open.

"I'd rather make you hard," she mewled, then slid around the door and into the back seat. "Don't give me time to change my mind," she purred, and I had no intention of letting the heat die down at all. I was going to enjoy this.

27

LILY

I lay down in the back seat of his car and snickered as he climbed in over me. I wasn't typically this spontaneous or adventurous, but I'd been so desperate to have some alone time with Ethan all week that this was the only thing that made sense. I knew he couldn't stay over. Mom and Dad were too old-fashioned. They'd flip out if they knew he was still here. And with Noah just coming home from the hospital, I couldn't stay at Ethan's house, either. This was our only shot.

"You're being frisky tonight," he growled as he pulled the door shut behind himself and grabbed me behind the knees, pulling me closer. I slid across the leather seat, giggling and reaching for him.

"It's been weeks. Shut up and kiss me." With my hands locked behind his head, I pulled him down and kissed him hard, tongues meeting and dancing together in a rhythm we'd come to know so well over the years. His hands slid under my shirt, up my back, and then around to cup my breasts. He moaned low in his throat as he broke the kiss and trailed his lips down my jaw line and along my collar bone.

"I've missed this," he mumbled against my skin. His hand slid further south, tracing along the insides of my thighs and making me shiver. His fingers were like fire as they brushed against me through my jeans. I threw my head back and arched toward him, willing him to touch me more.

"Tell me this is real..." I still couldn't wrap my mind around the idea that after all we'd been through, how I let him down and broke his heart, that he'd still want me.

"Yes, Lily, it's real." Ethan kissed me again, parting my lips to let his tongue trace along mine. I enjoyed him, relishing in the sensation of his hands smoothing across my skin. We were so in sync, nothing rushed, no moment too precious to savor.

"And you really love me and forgive me?" I asked as I spread my legs to allow him more room to settle closer to me. His weight pinned me against the leather, and I wrapped my legs around his hips.

"Lily, I've always loved you. I don't know how to not love you." Ethan looked into my eyes, and I saw the truth in his expression. His hands started to undo my jeans, and I pulled at his shirt, untucking it from his slacks. Any doubts I held evaporated with his words, and I felt emotion filling my chest.

My body warmed under his scorching touch, fingers tracing heat across my thighs as he slid my jeans and panties off. I tugged his shirt higher up around his chest so I could feel his skin beneath my palms and whimpered when he slipped a finger inside me.

"God, Lily, you're so wet," he groaned as his thumb started to rub my clit in time with his fingers moving inside me. My body arched off the seat, and I gasped as he slid a second finger into me, stretching me around him. Soon, he was pumping into me with an intensity that had me clawing at his back and moaning loudly, begging him for more.

"Shit, Ethan," I hissed, and I pushed his shoulders down. I wanted so much more.

As he backed across the seat, I scooted back too, sitting up and leaning against the door. I pulled my top off and tossed my bra as Ethan's mouth found my soaked valley. He kissed me there, lapping at my folds and swollen nub before sucking on it hard. Pleasure ripped through me.

"Ethan," I moaned, grabbing his hair as he continued his ministrations. His tongue was like fire against my core, teasing and shamelessly licking every drop of my arousal from my thighs. I gasped as he slid his index finger inside me again, hooking it upward and hitting that sweet spot. My toes curled and my hips jerked against him. I was so close to losing control.

I panted his name again as his mouth moved back up to my breasts, his fingers still buried deep inside me. His palm cupped my core while he suckled a red mark onto my skin. Ethan was good at what he did. I could barely catch my breath.

"Ethan, I'm gonna—" I arched my back and bit down on my bottom lip as the orgasm crashed over me, my body tensing and then releasing under him. He continued to lick and suckle at my breasts until the pleasure subsided and I was panting with exhaustion. His hand rubbed and thrust into me, and my pussy dripped onto his palm, slicking him, and when he was done, he sat back and licked his fingers clean. "Holy shit," I moaned, my chest heaving.

I heard his zipper slide down and then felt the car shake. When I opened my eyes, he was sitting on the seat with his pants around his ankles and his dick in hand, stroking. The look of hunger and emotion in his eyes drew me toward him. I rose up and knelt on the seat next to him, leaning with my hands on his shoulders as I lifted a leg and straddled him.

"I didn't bring a condom," I admitted, and he shrugged.

"I didn't either, but we don't need one." He tapped his dick on my mound, and I paused for a second. We'd done this a few times, the fuck and pull out bit. It was messy and sometimes left both of us wanting more, but if I wanted him, it was all we could do without a sleeve to prevent pregnancy.

"If you can wait, I can go get dressed and run up to my room and sneak back out." I kissed him as he grabbed one of my breasts and kneaded it, twisting a nipple. That always got me going.

"Lily," he said so softly I knew he had more to say. I paused and looked him in the eye. "I want to put babies in you. Lots of them. I want us to be a family. I want to marry you, and I want you and Noah to move in with me." His hand left my chest and cupped my cheek. "Please tell me you'll marry me."

Flooded with emotion, all I could do was nod at him. My eyes welled up, and I felt tears drip down my cheeks as I kissed him again and again. The slow pace of our lovemaking suddenly turned frantic as I rose up and he positioned himself at my entrance. I lowered my body inch by inch around his cock, and he filled me until it was almost so deep, it was painful.

"Yes," I whimpered, and I started grinding my pussy against him. "Okay, yes..." The thought of having another baby with him thrilled me, but not as much as the rest of his words. I would marry him and be with him because it was all I had ever wanted. He was what I wanted.

"Tell me you'll marry me again," he growled, and I nodded my head.

"Yes, yes, I'll marry you, Ethan."

His thrusts became more fervent, harder and deeper as he continued to angle his cock so that he hit that spot inside me. I threw my head back and moaned louder this time, gripping his shirt. The leather of the seats squeaked in time with our movements, and the car rocked. The windows fogged too, obscuring the view of what we were doing to the world beyond the glass. Our bodies became one, the serpentine rhythm of love the only dance we knew.

"Ethan, I'm there!" I cried out as another orgasm ripped through me, and he felt so fucking good inside me, pumping in and out of me. The friction of his cock gliding through my moisture was exquisite too, so much better than when he wore a condom. I never wanted to use condoms again, and I never wanted any man but him again. I convulsed and spasmed, milking him dry, and he bit down on one of my nipples and grunted as he neared his own climax.

"Fuck, Lily, I'm gonna come," he groaned into my ear before his hips bucked against me harder, his thrusts slowing, and his seed spilled inside me. The warmth of his explosion filled me, and I shuddered around him. My lips found his again, and I never wanted to stop kissing him. The world no longer existed for anyone but us.

SILVER FOX'S SECRET BABY

I draped myself over his chest and panted, and he wrapped his arms around me and pinned me against his flesh. His shirt had fallen, separating our skin, but just having him inside me and his arms around me was enough. I listened to his heavy breathing and tried to catch my breath.

"I mean it, Lily. I wasn't just saying that to push your buttons. I want you to marry me. I already spoke with your father. I just don't have a ring yet." Ethan kissed the top of my shoulder and then raked his teeth across my skin there.

I sat up and left my hands resting on his shoulder. I could feel his sex draining from my body, probably puddling around him on the seat, but he didn't seem to care. He was still hard, still pulsing inside me.

"I meant it too, Ethan. Yes, I want to marry you. I guess I just still don't believe this is true, like you have to pinch me or something so I know it's not a dream. I can't believe it." I smiled at him, and he pinched my ass hard. I winced and jumped up, and his cock slid from my body. "Ouch, hey. What was that!" I snickered, and he pushed me to the side where I collapsed on the seat next to him with a grin.

"You said pinch you," he joked, and he picked up my clothes and tossed them at me.

"Some proposal," I laughed and sighed happily. The rush of endorphins along with the week of very little sleep had me feeling drugged and yawning.

Ethan pulled his pants up and grimaced at me as he zipped up. "Gonna need a hot shower and the washing machine for these boxers."

"Ah, and probably a bigger house if you really did put more babies in me." I winked at him and sorted the clothing out to make sure I had the baby monitor turned up. The light glowed green, so I relaxed as I put on my panties and bra, then tugged my shirt over my head. I managed to get my jeans to my knees, but no higher in this cramped space.

Ethan opened the door and stood as a privacy barrier between me and the street as I shimmied them the rest of the way up before kissing him again. "That was exciting." I wrapped my arms around

169

LYDIA HALL

him and let him hold me in the same position leaning against the car as we had been in before I initiated sex.

"Yes, well I know you're a young whippersnapper, but this old man is kinda tired. I have to go home and sleep now."

I laughed at his corny joke and stepped back from him. "Good night, Ethan... Call me in the morning?"

He reached into the back seat and grabbed the baby monitor and handed it to me. "Wouldn't miss it. How about I bring donuts and coffee around eight?"

"Just coffee. Can't eat donuts in front of Noah while he's on his liquid diet. He can only have a protein breakfast shake." I grimaced and took the monitor out of his hand.

"Then milkshakes it is!" His triumphant announcement came complete with a fist raised in the air, and I had to laugh again.

"Alright, Dad. You need to slow down. The boy just had surgery, so I think nutrition is a better idea. But once he's all recovered, we can spoil him however you want." I pecked him on the cheek and sighed happily.

"Lily," Ethan said, taking my hand.

"Yeah?"

"Do you think he's going to adjust to my being his dad?" The sincere question melted my heart. Ethan was going to be such an amazing father. I couldn't wait to see him in action.

"I think he's going to love you every bit as much as I do, and years from now, we'll look back and there will be no evidence of your missing any part of his life except distant memories." His expression softened at my words.

"Goodnight, Lily."

"Night," I whispered, then I made my way back inside. My heart was full and giddy from the interaction. I was so restless, too, that I didn't want to lie down yet. I crept into Noah's room and turned the monitor off and sat in the rocking recliner in the corner near the night light to watch him sleeping.

Things were better than I ever hoped they'd be. Ethan and I were back on track, and Noah was on the road to recovery. It was like the heavens had opened and showered me in so much love and blessings, I couldn't even find the right place to start my thanks. I had a family, and it was whole again, and I couldn't be happier. Life really does have a way of working out, even when you least expect it.

28

EPILOGUE: ETHAN

The lights spun overhead, swirling and splashing across the dance floor. Noah ran past with a girl a few years older than him on his tails—literally. The tiny tuxedo looked adorable on him, and I was so happy that five months out from his surgery, he was back to his playful self and able to run and romp with the other kids at our reception.

Lily's hands were locked behind my neck, and she watched Noah race past too. She was so beautiful in her white gown with her hair swept up into a French twist with flowers pinned among her curls. We discarded the veil earlier in the night as our guests continuously tapped their forks on their glasses urging us to kiss. My lips were practically raw from all the kissing, and there would be more once we got to our condo in Orlando.

"He's going to have so much fun at Disney World," she said over the din of music playing through the speaker system.

"Yes, and he's going to wear us out. We're going to be the ones needing naps!" I chuckled, but it was true. Having a child so young at my age was a challenge already, and I only just started. Every day was such a journey, and I learned so much about love and patience.

"Your mom looks like she's waiting for you to ask her to dance,"

Lily said, nodding in the direction where Mom sat with a glass of wine in hand. She wore a sapphire dress suit and sat next to Dad, who looked tired. He hadn't been up on his feet much, but I was so thankful his physical therapy was going well enough for the nursing home to allow him to join us for the nuptials.

"Yes, she does." I pecked Lily on the cheek. "Mind if you have to share me for a dance or two, Mrs. Matthews?" I asked, and Lily grinned.

"I don't mind one bit, Mr. Matthews." She returned the kiss and backed away, and when our fingers lost touch, I turned and headed over to Mom. She smiled as I approached and set her glass down.

"Well, the old man hasn't asked you to dance yet tonight, I see." Dad rolled his eyes at my joke, but Mom reached out her hand.

"At least my strapping young son will spin me around the dance floor a time or two." I took her hand as she stood and turned to Dad.

"Sure you don't want to be the one sweeping this charming woman off her feet?" I asked, and he coughed a few times and waved me away. Healing physically from surgery was one thing, but the emotional toll he was under was still making him grumpy and distant. It would take time to help him feel normal again, but he would, as soon as he was fully autonomous again.

I led Mom to the dance floor, and she placed her hand on my shoulder and one in my palm as I guided her in a waltz. She still had the grace of a thirty-year-old, though she moved a bit more slowly now.

"So, are you ready for the move?" I asked. Lily and I had decided we wanted our whole family together. While her parents weren't quite ready to let go of their home and opted to stay put for now, we had purchased a large home on the north side of the city with enough room for both sets of our parents to stay with us. I hired a nursing company to begin at-home health care for Dad including a nurse who would stay at our home overnight to care for his needs as the rest of us slept. We were set to begin that when we returned from our honeymoon in Orlando.

"I'm a little nervous about the actual moving day, but I think it will turn out fine." Mom was pleased with the new place too. She was happy there were large flower gardens to work in, and Lily's mother promised to come by a couple of times a week to work on the land-scaping with her. I could afford a company to do it for us, but they were pleased as could be to have the freedom to put their hands in the soil.

"Ellen and David will be here to help with all of that. I'm sure you will all be just fine. The movers are professionals. And Lily and I already have most things boxed and labeled. It's just transporting everything over." When we planned the move, we both agreed it would be less stressful if we hired movers. Mom wasn't too happy, being from the generation that did everything themselves, but we managed to convince her that it would be okay.

"Well, I trust you," she said, patting my chest.

We talked about the move, then about Noah and how well he was doing. As we danced, Mom told me stories of my childhood, things I'd seen Noah doing that I never would have thought were inherited traits but to Mom, it was obvious. She and Dad loved my son as much as I did and almost as instantly. Noah was the only one for whom Dad would even smile currently, and it was like night and day. The boy had a way with my grumpy old dad.

When the song was over, I walked Mom back to her seat so she could be with Dad and noticed that Ellen and David were dancing with Noah. Lily stood near our table watching me. I made my way over to my blushing bride and took her into my arms with the inten-tion of not letting her go again tonight, and she covered her mouth and blinked at me.

"What's wrong?" I asked. She looked a little green, and right before our two-week trip to the happiest place on Earth with our little boy in tow. "Don't tell me you're coming down with something." Being November in Denver, it was definitely cold and flu season.

"Actually," she hummed, and she didn't sound at all sad or sick. "Remember when you told me that night in my parents' driveway that you wanted to put lots of babies in me?"

I reached to the corner of my mind and thought about what she was saying. I remembered the night I asked her to marry me and how I told her I wanted a family. I remembered her response too, eager to please me and accept my proposal, but that was five months ago. She'd have been showing by now. Unless...

"Don't tell me..." I pulled her against my body hard. "Really?" Lily nodded gleefully and practically glowed. "You're pregnant?"

"Yes, I am..."

"When? How?" I couldn't contain my happiness. I spun her around and kissed her hard, not even giving her a chance to respond right away. When I settled, she spoke.

"I've known for about a month now. I've been waiting until tonight to tell you. Since you decided to dispose of the condoms, it was inevitable." Her cute shrug made me want to eat her up.

"Mrs. Matthews, you have made me the happiest man alive. I can't believe how incredible you are. You're such a great mom, and I wouldn't want anyone else as my partner in life." I sighed contently. "Let's get out of here. We have to get Noah to sleep so we can get up early and catch our flight."

"Yes, let's. And buy me some Tums so I can stop feeling nauseous or the plane ride won't be so fun for me." She chuckled lightheartedly, and I spun her around one more time before taking her hand.

All my life, I dreamed of having a love like my parents'. The older I got, the less likely it seemed, but Lily Carter had made my dreams come true, even if the road had been a bit bumpy. And now we were embarking on the next leg of the journey, and I couldn't wait to experience all the bumps along the way.

Made in the USA
Monee, IL
13 February 2025

12106671R00111